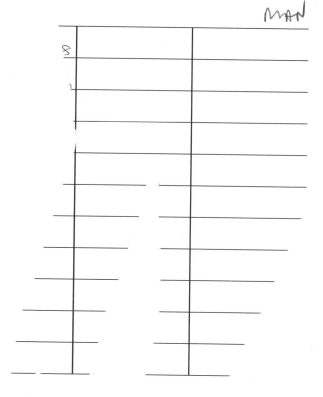

MAN

e ret   this b   or before the
. Tc   /g   w.essex .o
           2   to an

Paddington Children's Hospital

Caring for children—and captivating hearts!

The doctors and nurses of
Paddington Children's Hospital are renowned
for their expert care of their young patients,
no matter the cost. And now, facing both
a heart-wrenching emergency and
a dramatic fight to save their hospital,
the stakes are higher than ever!

Devoted to their jobs, these talented
professionals are about to discover that saving
lives can often mean risking your heart…

Available now in the thrilling
Paddington Children's Hospital miniseries:

Their One Night Baby
by Carol Marinelli

Forbidden to the Playboy Surgeon
by Fiona Lowe

Mummy, Nurse…Duchess?
by Kate Hardy

Falling for the Foster Mum
by Karin Baine

Healing the Sheikh's Heart
by Annie O'Neil

A Life-Saving Reunion
by Alison Roberts

Dear Reader,

How far back can you remember?

My earliest memory is of a pair of red shoes that I had when I was three years old—I still love red shoes!—and my love of big ships came from travelling from New Zealand to England when I was five years old. It took six weeks and I loved every minute of it!

I lived in London for eighteen months. My dad, who was a doctor, had a job at Hammersmith Hospital, and we lived in a basement apartment in Prince Albert Road—so close to the zoo that we could hear the animals at night sometimes. I started school there, and my favourite place to play was on Primrose Hill.

Setting a story in a place that was such an important part of my early life was such a treat and I even got to play in Regent's Park and on Primrose Hill again :)

Working with my talented colleagues at Mills & Boon Medical Romance has also been a treat. The threads in this series are very strong and so emotional that this was, at times, a heart-wrenching story to write.

What a privilege to bring those threads together and complete, not only a story that gives two people the chance of a love that will last for the rest of their lives, but also to celebrate the finale of all the other stories and the resolution of the conflict that runs through the Paddington Children's Hospital series.

Happy reading!

With love,

Alison

A LIFE-SAVING
REUNION

BY
ALISON ROBERTS

MILLS
BOON®

This is a work of fiction. Names, characters, places, locations and incidents are purely fictional and bear no relationship to any real life individuals, living or dead, or to any actual places, business establishments, locations, events or incidents. Any resemblance is entirely coincidental.

First published in Great Britain 2017
By Mills & Boon, an imprint of HarperCollins*Publishers*
1 London Bridge Street, London, SE1 9GF

Large Print edition 2017

© 2017 Harlequin Books S.A.

Special thanks and acknowledgement are given to Alison Roberts for her contribution to the Paddington Children's Hospital series.

ISBN: 978-0-263-06738-5

MIX
Paper from
responsible sources
FSC
www.fsc.org FSC™ C007454

This book is produced from independently certified FSC paper to ensure responsible forest management. For more information visit www.harpercollins.co.uk/green.

Printed and bound in Great Britain
by CPI Group (UK) Ltd, Croydon, CR0 4YY

Alison Roberts is a New Zealander, currently lucky enough to be living in the south of France. She is also lucky enough to write for the Mills & Boon Medical Romance line. A primary school teacher in a former life, she is also a qualified paramedic. She loves to travel and dance, drink champagne, and spend time with her daughter and her friends.

Books by Alison Roberts

Mills & Boon Medical Romance

Christmas Eve Magic

Their First Family Christmas

Wildfire Island Docs

The Nurse Who Stole His Heart
The Fling That Changed Everything

A Little Christmas Magic
Always the Midwife
Daredevil, Doctor...Husband?

Mills & Boon Cherish

The Wedding Planner and the CEO
The Baby Who Saved Christmas
The Forbidden Prince

Visit the Author Profile page
at millsandboon.co.uk for more titles.

CHAPTER ONE

HE'D KNOWN THIS wasn't going to be easy.

He'd known that some cases were going to be a lot harder than others.

But Dr Thomas Wolfe had also known that, after the very necessary break, he had been ready to go back to the specialty that had always been his first love.

Paediatric cardiology.

Mending broken little hearts...

And some not so little, of course. Paddington Children's Hospital cared for an age range from neonates to eighteen-year-olds. After dealing only with adults for some years now, Thomas was probably more comfortable interacting with the adolescents under his care here but he'd more than rediscovered his fascination with babies in the last few months. And the joy of the children who were old enough to understand how sick they were, brave kids who could teach a lot of people things about dealing with life.

Or kids that touched your heart and made doing the best job you possibly could even more of a priority. It had to be carefully controlled, mind you. If you let yourself get too close, it could not only affect your judgement, but it could also end up threatening to destroy you.

And Thomas Wolfe wasn't about to let that happen again.

He had to pause for a moment, standing in the central corridor of Paddington's cardiology ward, right beside the huge, colourful cut-outs of Pooh Bear and friends that decorated this stretch of wall between the windows of the patients' rooms. Tigger seemed to be grinning down at him— mid-bounce—as Thomas pretended to read a new message on his pager.

This had become the hardest case since he'd returned to Paddington's. A little girl who made it almost impossible to keep a safe distance. Six-year-old Penelope Craig didn't just touch the hearts of people who came to know her. She grabbed it with both hands and squeezed so hard it was painful.

It wasn't that he needed a moment to remind himself how important it was to keep that distance, because he had been honing those skills from the moment he'd stepped back through the doors of this astonishing, old hospital and they were already ingrained enough to be automatic. He just needed to make sure the guardrails were completely intact because if there was a weak area, Penny would be the one to find it and push through.

And that couldn't be allowed to happen.

With a nod, as if he'd read an important message on his pager, Thomas lifted his head and began moving towards the nearest door. There was no hesitation as he tapped to announce his arrival and then entered the room with a smile.

His smile faltered for a split second as Julia Craig, Penny's mother, caught his gaze with the unspoken question that was always there now.

Is today the day?

His response was as silent as the query.

No. Today's not the day.

The communication was already well practised enough to be no slower than the blink of an eye. Penny certainly hadn't noticed.

'Look, Dr Wolfe! I can dance.'

The fact that Penny was out of her bed meant that today was one of her better ones. She still had her nasal cannula stuck in place with a piece of sticky tape on each cheek, the long plastic tube snaking behind her to where it connected with the main oxygen supply, but she was on her feet.

No, she was actually standing on her tippy-toes, her arms drooping gracefully over the frill of her bright pink tutu skirt. And then she tried to turn in a circle but the tubing got in the way and she lost her balance and sat down with a suddenness that might have upset many children.

Penny just laughed.

'Oops.' Julia scooped her daughter into her arms as the laughter turned to gasping.

'I can…' Penny took another gulp of air. 'I *can*…do it. Watch!'

'Next time.' Julia lifted Penny onto her bed. 'Dr Wolfe is here to see you and he's very busy. He's got lots of children to look after today.'

'But only one who can dance.' Thomas smiled. 'Just like a Ballerina Bear.'

Penny's smile could light up a room. Big grey eyes turned their attention to the television on the wall, where her favourite DVD was playing and a troupe of fluffy bears wearing tutus were performing what seemed to be a cartoon version of *Swan Lake*.

'I just want to listen to your heart, if that's okay.' Thomas unhooked his stethoscope from around his neck.

Penny nodded but didn't turn away from the screen. She lifted her arms above her head and curled her finger as she tried to mimic the movements of the dancing bears.

Thomas noted the bluish tinge to his small patient's lips. Putting the disc of his stethoscope against a chest scarred by more than one major surgery, he listened to a heart that was trying its best to pump enough blood around a small body but failing a little more each day.

The new medication regime was helping but it wasn't enough. Penny had been put on the waiting list for a heart transplant weeks ago and the job of Thomas and his team was to keep her healthy for long enough that the gift of a long life might be possible. It was a balancing act of drugs to help her heart pump more effectively and control the things that made it harder, like the build-up of fluid in her tissues and lungs. Limiting physical activity was unfortunately a necessity now, as well, and to move further than this room required that Penny was confined to a wheelchair.

The odds of a heart that was a good match becoming available in time weren't great but, as heartbreaking as that was, it wasn't why this particular case was proving so much more difficult than other patients he had on the waiting list for transplants.

Penny was a direct link to his past.

The past he'd had to walk away from in order to survive.

He'd met Penny more than six years ago. Before she was even born, in fact—when ultrasound tests had revealed that the baby's heart had one of the most serious congenital defects it could have, with the main pumping chamber too small to be effective. She'd had her first surgery when she was only a couple of weeks old and he'd been the doctor looking after her both before and after that surgery.

He'd spent a lot of time with Penny's parents, Julia and Peter Craig, and he'd felt their anguish as acutely as if it had been his own.

That was what becoming a parent yourself could do to you...

Gwen had only been a couple of years older than Penny so she would have been eight now. Would she have fallen in love with the Ballerina Bears, too? Be going to ballet lessons, perhaps, and wearing a pink tutu on top of any other clothing, including her pyjamas?

The thought was no more than a faint, mental jab. Thomas had known that working with children again might stir up the contents of that locked vault in his head and his heart but he knew how to deal with it.

He knew to step away from the danger zone.

He stepped away from the bed, too. 'It's a lovely day, today,' he said, looping the stethoscope around his neck again. 'Maybe Mummy can take you outside into the sunshine for a bit.'

A nurse came into the room as he spoke and he glanced at the kidney dish in one hand and a glass of juice in the other. 'After you've had all your pills.'

'Are you in a rush?' Julia was on her feet, as well. 'Have you got a minute?' She glanced at her daughter, who was still entranced by the dancing bears on the screen. 'I'll be back in a minute, Penny. Be a good girl and swallow all those pills for Rosie, okay?'

''kay.' Penny nodded absently.

'Of course she will,' Rosie said. 'And then I want to know all the names of those bears, again. Who's the one with the sparkly blue fur?'

'Sapphire,' Thomas could hear Penny saying as he held the door open for Julia. If she had concerns about her daughter's condition, they needed to go somewhere else to discuss it. 'She's my favourite. And the green one's Emerald and…the red one's Ruby…'

The relatives' room a little further down the corridor was empty. Thomas closed the door behind them and gestured for Julia to take one of the comfortable chairs available.

'Are you sure you've got time?'

'Of course.'

'I just… I just wanted to ask you more about what you said yesterday. I tried to explain to Peter last night but I think I made it sound a lot worse than…than you did…' Julia was fighting tears now.

Thomas nudged the box of tissues on the coffee table closer and Julia gratefully pulled several out.

'You mean the ventricular assist device?'

Julia nodded, the wad of tissues pressed to her face.

'You said...you said it would be the next step, when...*if*...things got worse.'

Thomas kept his tone gentle. 'They sound scary, I know, but it's something that's often used as a bridge to transplant. For when heart failure is resistant to medical therapy, the way Penny's is becoming.'

'And you said it might make her a lot better in the meantime?'

'It can improve circulation and can reverse some of the other organ damage that heart failure can cause.'

'But it's risky, isn't it? It's major surgery...'

'I wouldn't suggest it if the risks of going on as we are were less than the risks of the surgery. I know Penny's having a better day today but you already know how quickly that can change and it gets a little more difficult to control every time.'

Julia blew her nose. 'I know. That last time

she had to go to intensive care, we thought…we thought we were going to lose her…'

'I know.' Thomas needed to take in a slow breath. To step away mentally and get back onto safe ground. Professional ground.

'A VAD could make Penny more mobile again and improve her overall condition so that when a transplant becomes available, the chances of it being successful are that much higher. It's a longer term solution to control heart failure and they can last for years, but yes, it is a major procedure. The device is attached to the heart and basically takes over the work of the left ventricle by bypassing it. Let's make a time for me to sit down with both you and Peter and I can talk you through it properly.'

Julia had stopped crying. Her eyes were wide.

'What do you mean by "more mobile"? Would we be able to take her home again while we wait?'

'I would hope so.' Thomas nodded. 'She would be able to go back to doing all the things she would normally do at home. Maybe more, even.'

Julia had her fingers pressed against her lips.

Her voice was no more than a whisper. 'Like… like dancing lessons, maybe?'

Oh…he had to look away from that hope shining through the new tears in Julia's eyes. The wall of the relatives' room was a much safer place.

'I'll tell Peter when he comes in after work. How soon can we make an appointment to talk about it?'

'Talk to Maria on the ward reception desk. She seems to know my diary as well as I do.' He got to his feet, still not risking a direct glance at Julia's face.

From the corner of his eye, he could see Julia turn her head. Was she wondering what had caught his attention?

He was being rude. He turned back to his patient's mother but now Julia was staring at the wall.

'My life seems to be full of teddy bears,' she said.

Thomas blinked at the random comment. 'Oh? You mean the dancing kind?'

'And here, look. This is about the Teddy Bears'

Picnic in Regent's Park. Well, Primrose Hill, actually. For transplant families.'

The poster had only been a blur of colour on the wall but now Thomas let his gaze focus.

And then he wished he hadn't.

Right in the middle of a bright collage of photos was one of a surgeon, wearing green theatre scrubs, with a small child in her arms. The toddler was wearing only a nappy so the scar down the centre of her chest advertised her major cardiac surgery. The angelic little girl, with her big, blue eyes and mop of golden curls, was beaming up at her doctor and the answering smile spoke of both the satisfaction of saving a small life and a deep affection for her young patient.

'That's Dr Scott,' Julia said. 'Rebecca. But you know that, of course.'

Of course he did.

'She did the surgery on Penny when she was a baby—but you know that too. How silly of me. You were her doctor back then, too.' Julia made an apologetic face. 'So much has happened since then, it becomes a bit of a blur, sometimes.'

'Yes.' Thomas was still staring at Rebecca's face. Those amazing dark, chocolate-coloured eyes which had been what had caught his attention first, all those years ago, when he'd spotted her in one of his classes at medical school. The gleaming, straight black hair that was wound up into a knot on the back of her head, the way it always was when she was at work.

That smile…

He hadn't seen her look that happy since…well, since before their daughter had died.

She certainly hadn't shown him even a hint of a smile like that in the months since he'd returned to Paddington's.

Had Julia not realised they had been husband and wife at the time they'd shared Penny's care in the weeks after her birth?

Well, why would she? They had kept their own names to avoid any confusion at work and they'd always been completely professional during work hours. Friendly professional, though—nothing like the strained relationship between them now. And Julia and Peter had had far more on their minds than how close a couple of people were amongst the team of medics trying to save their tiny daughter.

'She was just a surgeon, back then.'

Thomas had to bite back a contradiction. Rebecca had never been 'just' a surgeon. She'd been talented and brilliant and well on the way to a stellar career from the moment she'd graduated from medical school.

'Isn't it amazing that she's gone on to specialise in transplants?'

'Mmm.' Sometimes the traumatic events that happened in life could push you in a new direction but Thomas couldn't say that out loud, either. If Julia didn't know about the personal history that might have prompted the years of extra study to add a new field of expertise to Rebecca's qualifications, he was the last person who would enlighten her.

Sharing something like that was an absolute no-no when you were keeping a professional distance from patients and their families. And from your ex-wife.

'It's amazing for us, anyway,' Julia continued. 'Because it means that she'll be able to do Penny's transplant if we're lucky enough to find a new heart for her...' Her voice wobbled. 'It might be us going to one of these picnics next year. I've heard of them. Did you see the programme on telly a while back, when they had all those people talking about how terrible it would be if Paddington's got closed?'

'I don't think I did.' The media coverage over the threatened closure had become so intense it had been hard to keep up with it all, especially since Sheikh Al Khalil had announced last month that he would be donating a substantial sum of money following his daughter's surgery.

'Well, they had a clip from last year's picnic. They were talking to a mother who had lost her child through some awful accident and she had made his organs available for transplant. She said she'd never been brave enough to try and make contact with the families of the children who had received them, but she came to the picnic and imagined that someone there might be one of them. She watched them running their races and playing games and saw how happy they were. And how happy their families were...'

Julia had to stop because she was crying again, even though she was smiling. Thomas was more than relieved. He couldn't have listened any longer. He was being dragged into a place he never went these days if he could help it.

'I really must get on with my rounds,' he said.

'Of course. I'm so sorry...' Julia had another handful of tissues pressed to her nose as he opened the door of the relatives' room so she could step out before him.

'It's not a problem,' Thomas assured her. 'I'm always here to talk to you. And Peter, of course. Let's set up that appointment to talk about the ventricular assist device very soon.'

Julia nodded, but her face crumpled again as her thoughts clearly returned to something a lot less happy than the thought of attending a picnic to celebrate the lives that had been so dramatically improved by the gift of organ donation. The urge to put a hand on her shoulder to comfort her and offer reassurance was so strong, he had to curl his fingers into a fist to stop his hand moving.

'Um…' Thomas cleared his throat. 'Would you like me to find someone to sit with you for a bit?'

Julia shook her head. 'I'll be fine. You go. I'll just get myself together a bit more before I go back to Penny. I don't want her to see that I've been crying.'

Even a view of only the woman's back was enough to advertise her distress, but it was the body language of the man standing so rigidly beside her that caught Dr Rebecca Scott's attention instantly as she stepped out of the elevator to head towards the cardiology ward at the far end of the corridor.

A sigh escaped her lips and her steps slowed a little as she fought the impulse to spin around and push the button to open the lift doors again. To go somewhere else. It wasn't really an option. She had a patient in the cardiology ward who was on the theatre list for tomorrow morning and she knew that the parents were in need of a lot of reassurance. This small window of time in her busy day was the only slot available so she would just have to lift her chin and deal with having her path cross with that of her ex-husband.

How sad was it that she'd known it was Thomas simply because of the sense of disconnection with the person he was talking to?

He might have returned to work at Paddington's but the Thomas Wolfe that Rebecca had known and loved hadn't come back.

Oh, he still looked the same. Still lean and fit and so tall that the top of her head would only reach his shoulder. He still had those eyes that had fascinated her right from the start because they could change colour depending on his mood. Blue when he was happy and grey when he was angry or worried or sad.

They had been the colour of a slate roof on a rainy day that first time they had seen each other again after so long and she hadn't noticed any difference since. He was as aloof with her as he was with his patients and their families.

She'd known it wasn't going to be easy. She'd known that some cases were going to be a lot harder than others but, when she'd heard that he'd agreed to come back and work at Paddington's, Rebecca had believed that she could cope. She'd wondered if they could, in fact, put some of the past behind them and salvage some kind of friendship, even.

That hope had been extinguished the first time their paths had crossed when nothing had been said. When there had been no more warmth in his gaze than if she'd been any other colleague he'd previously worked with.

Less warmth, probably.

The old Thomas had never been like that. He'd had an easy grin that was an invitation for colleagues to stop and chat for a moment or two. He would joke and play with the children in his care and he'd always had a knack for connecting with parents—especially after he'd become a father himself. They loved him because he could make them feel as if they had the best person possible fighting in their corner. Someone who understood exactly how hard it was and would care for their child as if it were his own.

This version of Thomas might have the same—or likely an improved—ability to deliver the best medical care but he was a shell of the man he had once been.

Part of Rebecca's heart was breaking for a man who'd taught himself to disconnect so effectively from the people around him but, right now, an even bigger part was angry. Maybe it had been building with every encounter they'd had over the last few months when they had discussed the care of their patients with a professional respect that bordered on coldness.

Calling each other 'Thomas' and 'Rebecca' with never a single slip into the 'Tom' and 'Becca' they had always been to each other. Discussing test results and medications and surgery as if nobody involved had a personal life or people that loved them enough to be terrified.

It was bad enough that he'd destroyed their marriage by withdrawing into this cold, hard shell but she could deal with that. She'd had years of practice, after all. To see the effect it was having on others made it far less acceptable. This was Penny's mother he'd been talking to, for heaven's sake. They'd both known Julia since she'd been pregnant with her first—and only—child. They'd both been there for her a thousand per cent over the first weeks and months of her daughter's life. He'd been the old Thomas, then.

And then he'd walked out. He hadn't been there for the next lot of surgery Penny had had. He hadn't shared the joy of appointments over the next few years that had demonstrated how well the little girl had been and how happy and hopeful her family was. He hadn't been there to witness the fear returning as her condition had deteriorated again but now he was back on centre stage and he was acting as if Penelope Craig was just another patient. As if he had no personal connection at all…

How could he be walking away from Julia like that, when she was so upset she had buried her face in a handful of tissues, ducking back into the relatives' room for some privacy?

Rebecca's forward movement came to a halt as Thomas came closer. She knew she was glaring at him but, for once, she wasn't going to hide anything personal behind a calm, professional mask.

'What's going on?' she asked, her tone rather more crisp than she had expected. 'Why is Julia so upset?'

Thomas shifted his gaze, obviously checking that nobody was within earshot. A group of both staff and visitors were waiting for an elevator. Kitchen staff went past, pushing a huge stainless steel trolley. An orderly pushing a bed came towards them, heading for the service lift, presumably taking the small patient for an X-ray or scan. The bed had balloons tied to the end, one of them a bright yellow smiley face. A nurse walked beside the bed, chatting to the patient's mother. She saw Rebecca and smiled. Then her gaze shifted to Thomas and the smile faded a little.

He didn't seem to notice. He tilted his head towards the group of comfortable chairs near the windows that were, remarkably, free of anyone needing a break or waiting to meet someone. Far enough away from the elevator doors to allow for a private conversation.

Fair enough. It would be unprofessional to discuss details of a case where it could be overheard. Rebecca followed his lead but didn't sit down on one of the chairs. Neither did Thomas.

'I was going to send you a memo,' he said. 'I'm meeting both Julia and Peter in the next day or two to discuss the option of Penelope receiving a ventricular assist device. It's only a matter of time before her heart failure becomes unmanageable.'

'Okay…' Rebecca caught her bottom lip between her teeth. No wonder Julia had been upset. A VAD was a major intervention. But she trusted Thomas's judgement and it would definitely buy them some time.

His gaze touched hers for just a heartbeat as he finished speaking but Rebecca found herself staring at his face, waiting for him to look at her again. Surely he could understand the effect of what he'd told Julia? How could he have walked away from her like that and left her alone?

But Thomas seemed to be scanning the view

of central London that these big, multi-paned old windows provided. He could probably see the busy main roads with their red, double-decker buses and crowds of people waiting at intersections or trying to hail a black cab. Or maybe his eye had been drawn to the glimpse of greenery in the near distance from the treetops of Regent's Park.

'You've had experience with VADs? Are you happy to do the surgery?'

'Yes, of course. It's not a procedure that happens very often but I've been involved with a couple. Do you want me to come to the meeting with Penny's family and discuss it with them?'

'Let's wait until it's absolutely necessary. I can tell them what's involved and why it's a good option.'

Rebecca let her gaze shift to the windows, as well. She stepped closer, in fact, and looked down. The protesters were still in place, with their placards, outside the gates. They'd been there for months now, ever since the threat of closure had been made public. It hadn't just been the staff who had been so horrified that the land value of this prime central London spot was so high that the board of governors was actually considering selling up and merging Paddington Children's Hospital with another hospital, Riverside, that was outside the city limits.

Thanks to the incredible donation a month or so ago from Sheikh Idris Al Khalil, who'd brought his daughter to Paddington's for treatment, the threat of closure was rapidly retreating. The astonishing amount of money in appreciation of such a successful result for one child had sparked off an influx of new donations and the press were onside with every member of staff, every patient and every family who were so determined that they would stay here. Even so, the protesters were not going to let the momentum of their campaign slow down until success was confirmed. The slogans on their placards were as familiar as the street names around here now.

Save Our Hospital
Kids' Health Not Wealth

The knowledge that that announcement couldn't be far off gave Rebecca a jolt of pleasure. Things were looking up. For Paddington's and maybe for Penny, too.

'It is a good option.' She nodded. 'I'd love to see her out of that wheelchair for a while.'

'It would put her at the top of the waiting list for a new heart, too. Hopefully a donor heart will become available well before we run into any complications.'

The wave of feeling positive ebbed, leaving Rebecca feeling a kind of chill run down her spine. Her muscles tensed in response. Her head told her that she should murmur agreement and then excuse herself to go and see her patient, maybe adding a polite request to be kept informed of any developments.

Her heart was sending a very different message. An almost desperate cry asking where the hell had the man gone that Thomas used to be? Was there even a fragment of him left inside that shell?

'Yes,' she heard herself saying, her voice weirdly

low and fierce. 'Let's keep our fingers crossed that some kid somewhere, who's about the same age as Penny, has a terrible accident and their parents actually agree to have him—or *her*—used for spare parts.'

She could feel the shock wave coming from Thomas. She was shocked herself.

It was a pretty unprofessional thing for a transplant surgeon to say but this had come from a very personal place. A place that only a parent who had had to make that heartbreaking decision themselves could understand.

She was also breaking the unspoken rule that nothing personal existed between herself and Thomas any more. And she wasn't doing it by a casually friendly comment like 'How are you?' or 'Did you have a good weekend?' No. She was lobbing a verbal grenade into the bunker that contained their most private and painful history.

In public. During working hours.

What *was* she thinking? Being angry at the distance Thomas was keeping himself from his patients and their parents was no excuse. Especially when she knew perfectly well why he had become like that. Or was that the real issue here? That she had known and tried so hard to help and had failed so completely?

'Sorry,' she muttered. 'But, for me, it's never an anonymous donor organ that becomes available. I have to go and collect them so I get involved in both sides of the story.'

Thomas's voice was like ice. He really didn't want to be talking about this.

'You *choose* to do it,' he said.

He didn't even look at her as he fired the accusation. He was staring out of the damned window again. Rebecca found that her anger hadn't been erased by feeling ashamed of her outburst.

'And you choose to shut your eyes.' The words came out in a whisper that was almost a hiss. 'To run away. Like you always did.'

There was no point in saying anything else. Maybe there was nothing more to say, anyway.

So Rebecca turned and walked away.

CHAPTER TWO

'THE LINE HAS been crossed.'

'Oh?' Thomas had opened the file he needed on his laptop. He clicked on options to bring his PowerPoint presentation up and sync it to the wall screen he had lowered over the whiteboard in this small meeting room. 'What line is that, Rosie?'

He certainly knew what line had been crossed as far as he was concerned. It had been a week since Rebecca's astonishing outburst and he still hadn't recovered from the shock of how incredibly unprofessional she had been.

What if someone had overheard? Members of the press were still all over any story coming out of Paddington's. Imagine a headline that revealed that the leading transplant surgeon of Paddington

Children's Hospital described her donor organs as 'spare parts'?

Anyone else could well have taken the matter elsewhere. Filed a formal complaint, even. And was Rosie now referring to it? Had it somehow made its way onto the hospital grapevine?

No. Her expression was far too happy to suggest a staff scandal. He tuned back in to what she was saying.

'...and now that the bottom line's been crossed, thanks to the flood of donations, the government's stepping in to make up any shortfall. It only needs the signature of the Minister of Health and Paddington's will be officially safe. There won't be any merger.'

'That's good news.' Thomas reached for the laser pointer in its holder on the frame of the whiteboard. '*Very* good news,' he added, catching sight of Rosie's disappointment in his lack of enthusiasm.

'Mmm.' Rosie looked unconvinced. 'Apparently there's going to be a huge party organised in the near future as soon as everything's finally signed and sealed but some of the staff are planning to get together at the Frog and Peach over the road on Friday to celebrate early. Guess we'll see you there?'

She was smiling but didn't wait for a response. Other people were arriving for the meeting now and there were bound to be far more acceptable reactions from anyone who hadn't heard the big news of the day. One of the physiotherapists, perhaps. Or Louise, who was the head dietician for Paddington's. One of the staff psychologists had just come in, too, and Thomas nodded a greeting to the head of the cardiac intensive care unit, who came through the door immediately after her.

Everybody in the team who had—or would be—directly involved in Penelope Craig's case had been invited to this meeting, including Rosie as one of the nurses that had provided so much of her care over the many admissions the little girl had had. One of the only people missing as the clock clicked onto the start time of eleven a.m. was her surgeon.

Rebecca Scott.

He hadn't seen her all week, come to think of it. Not that he'd wanted their paths to cross. The shock of their last interaction hadn't been only due to her lack of professionalism. Or that she had so unexpectedly crossed the boundaries of what their new relationship allowed.

No. Thomas had not been able to shake the echo of that vehement parting shot. That he chose to shut his eyes. To run away. And that he had always made that choice.

Did she really think he was such a coward?

He *wasn't* a coward. Had Rebecca had no understanding of how much strength it had taken to deal with what they had gone through? How hard it had been to keep putting one foot in front of the other and keep going?

Obviously not.

No wonder their marriage had fallen apart so easily.

No wonder he had been left feeling such a failure. As a husband *and* as a father.

But to drag it out again and hurl it in his face like that…

It had been uncalled for. Unhelpful. Insulting, even.

And so, yes, he was angry.

'Sorry we're late…' The door opened as Rebecca rushed in to take a seat at the oval table, followed by her senior registrar.

Thomas could feel himself glaring at the late arrivals.

Rebecca was glaring right back at him. 'We got held up in Recovery after our last case. I couldn't leave until I was sure my patient was stable.'

'Of course you couldn't,' someone said. 'We wouldn't expect you to.'

Thomas looked away first. Just in time to notice the raised eyebrows and shared glances that went round the table like a Mexican wave.

'No problem,' he said evenly. 'But let's get started, shall we? We're *all* busy people.'

The tension in the room behind him felt like an additional solid presence as he faced the screen and clicked the pointer to bring up his first slide.

'As you know, we're here to discuss a case we're all involved with—that of Penelope Craig, who's currently an inpatient in our cardiology ward. For those of you who haven't been so directly involved in the last few years, though, here's a quick case history.'

The slide was a list of bullet points. A summary of a clinical case reduced to succinct groups of words that made one crisis after another no more than markers on a timeline.

'The diagnosis of hypoplastic left heart syndrome was made prenatally so Penelope was delivered by C-section and admitted directly to the cardiac intensive care unit. She underwent her first surgery—a Norwood procedure—at thirteen days old.'

He had been in the gallery to watch that surgery. Rebecca had been a cardiothoracic surgical registrar at the time and it had been the most challenging case she'd assisted with. She'd sat up half the previous night as she'd gone over and over the steps of the surgery and Thomas had stayed up with her, trying to make up for any lack of confidence she was feeling. Even as he paused only long enough to take a breath, the flash of another memory came up like a crystal-clear video clip.

He had been in the front row of the gallery, leaning forward as he looked down at the tiny figure on the operating table and the group of gowned and masked people towering over it. Over the loudspeaker, he had heard the consultant surgeon hand over the responsibility of closing the tiny chest to Rebecca. As they changed positions, she had glanced up for a split second and caught Thomas's gaze through the glass window—as if to reassure herself that he was still there. That he was still with her with every step she took. And he had smiled and nodded, giving her the silent message that he believed in her. That she could do this and do it well.

That he was proud of her...

His voice sounded oddly tight as he continued. 'A hemi-Fontan procedure was done at six months to create a direct connection between the pulmonary artery and the superior vena cava.'

Rebecca had been allowed to do most of that procedure and she'd been so quietly proud of herself. They'd found a babysitter for Gwen and they'd gone out to celebrate the achievement with dinner and champagne and a long, delicious twirl around the dance floor of their favourite restaurant.

Those 'date' nights had always had a particular kind of magic. It didn't matter how frantic the hours and days before them had been or how tired they were when they set out. Somehow they could always tap back into the connection that had been there from their very first date—that feeling that their love for each other was invincible. That there could never be anyone else that they would want to be with.

The idea that the night after that surgery would be the last 'date' night they would ever have would have been unthinkable at the time. As impossible as losing their precious child.

Thomas didn't actually know if it had been Rebecca who had done the final major surgery to try and improve the function of Penelope's heart.

He'd walked out by then, taking a new job in adult cardiology at a major hospital up north in the wake of that personal tragedy that had torn their lives apart.

He'd run away...like he always did...

Thomas cleared his throat as he rapidly ran through the list of the more recent admissions.

'April of this year saw a marked deterioration in Penelope's condition following a series of viral infections. She's been an inpatient for the last ten weeks and was placed on the waiting list for a heart transplant about two months ago. This last week has seen a further deterioration in her condition and there's an urgent need for intervention.'

The next slide was a set of statistics about the availability of transplant organs and how many young patients were unlikely to make it as far as receiving a new heart.

The slide after that sombre reminder was a picture of a device that looked like a tiny rubber plunger with a single tube attached to the top and two coming out from the base.

'For those of you not familiar with these, this is a ventricular assist device—an implantable form of mechanical circulatory support. Parental consent has been given and it's our plan for Penelope to receive a VAD as soon as theatre time can be arranged.' Thomas sucked in a longer breath. 'Dr Scott? Perhaps you'd like to speak about what the surgery involves?'

Using her formal title caused another round of those raised eyebrows and significant glances. Was it his imagination or did this meeting feel really awkward for everybody here?

'Of course.' Rebecca's gaze quickly scanned everybody at the table. It just didn't shift to include himself. 'To put it simply, it's a straightforward bit of plumbing, really. The device is a pump that uses the apex of the left ventricle as the inflow and provides an outflow to the aorta, bypassing the ventricle that's not functioning well enough.'

Thomas could feel himself frowning. It was fine to describe something in layman's terms for the members of the team with no medical background, like the dietician and the psychologist, but to his own ears it was simple enough to be almost dismissive. Like describing a donor organ as a spare part?

His anger had settled into his stomach like a heavy stone. No wonder he hadn't been that interested in eating in the last few days. Was it going to get even worse when he had to work so closely with Rebecca on Penelope's case? Perhaps the unwanted memories that had ambushed him during his brief presentation had been a warning that it was going to become increasingly difficult to work with his ex-wife. The prospect was more than daunting, especially given that everybody else here seemed to be aware of the tension between them.

David, the cardiac intensive care consultant, was giving him a speculative glance as if he was also having concerns about how this particular combination of the lead carers in this team was going to work. With an effort, Thomas erased the unimpressed lines from his face.

'Of course it's not quite that simple in reality,'

Rebecca continued. 'It's a big and potentially difficult surgery and there are complications that we have to hope we'll avoid.'

'Like what?' The query came from one of the physiotherapists.

'Bleeding. Stroke. Infections. Arrhythmias.' Rebecca was counting off the possible disasters on her fingers. 'Some might not become apparent immediately, like renal failure and liver dysfunction. And some intraoperative ones, like an air embolism, are things we will certainly do our best to control. I guess what I'm trying to say is that there *are* risks but everybody agrees that the potential benefits outweigh these risks in Penny's case.'

Rebecca's smile was poignant. 'As most of you know, Penny Craig is one of those patients you just can't help falling in love with and we've known her all her life.

'I'm sure we're all going to give this case everything we've got.' Her smile wobbled a fraction. 'I know *I* am...'

The murmur of agreement around the table

held a note of involvement that was very unusual for a clinical team meeting like this. Heads were nodding solemnly. Rosie was blinking as if she was trying to fight back tears.

For heaven's sake… Did nobody else understand how destructive it could be to get too involved? Was the staff psychologist taking this atmosphere on board and making a mental note that a lot of people might need some counselling in the not-too-distant future if things *didn't* work out the way they all had their hearts set on?

Thomas raised his voice. 'It's certainly all about teamwork and it's to be hoped that we will see a dramatic improvement in this patient's condition within a very short period of time.' He glanced down at the laser pointer in his hand, looking for the 'off' button. 'Thank you all for coming. I look forward to working with everybody.'

A buzz of conversation broke out and more than one pager sounded. David came around to his end of the table. 'I'm being paged to get back upstairs but come and see me when you have a moment? I'd like to go over the postoperative care for Penny in some more detail so I can brief my staff.'

'Sure. I'll be heading up there shortly. There's a four-year-old who was admitted to ICU with severe asthma last night but now they're querying cardiomyopathy. We might need to transfer her to your patch.'

'I heard about that. Page me if you need me in on that consult.'

'Will do.'

The rest of the room was emptying during the brief conversation with David. Everybody had urgent tasks waiting for them elsewhere, including himself. Thomas shut down the programme on his laptop and picked it up, his thoughts already on the case he was about to go and assess. Severe breathlessness and wheezing in children could often be misdiagnosed as asthma or pneumonia until more specific tests such as echocardiography were used to reveal underlying heart disease.

It was a complete surprise to turn and find he was not alone in the room.

Rebecca was standing at the other end of the table.

'We need to talk,' she said.

Thomas said nothing. Given how disturbing their last private conversation had been, he wasn't at all sure he wanted an opportunity that could, in fact, make things worse.

'I'm sure you agree that we can't work together with this kind of tension between us. Especially not on a case like this. Everybody's aware of it and it's destructive to the whole team.'

He couldn't argue with that. And, to his shame, he knew he had to take part of the blame. He had no reason to feel angry with Rebecca for anything to do with her involvement in Penelope's case. He was letting personal baggage affect his relationship with a colleague to such an extent, it was actually difficult to make eye contact with her right now.

He looked down at the laptop in his hands.

'So what do you suggest? That we call in a different cardiologist? In case you hadn't noticed, they've been short-staffed around here ever since the threat of the merger got real. That's why I agreed to take on a permanent position again.'

A brief upwards glance showed that Rebecca's gaze was on him. Steady and unrelenting. He held her gaze for a heartbeat. And then another as those dark eyes across the length of the table merged with that flash of memory he'd had during his presentation—when they'd been looking up at him for reassurance that she had his support when she'd been facing one of her biggest challenges.

A different lifetime.

One in which giving and receiving that kind of reassurance and support had been as automatic as breathing. When success for either of them had created a shared pride so huge it could make it hard to catch a breath and when failure was turned into a learning experience that could only make you a better person. A lifetime that had been iced with so much laughter.

So much love…

It had been a long time since that loss had kicked him quite this hard. A wave of sadness blurred the edges of any anger he still had.

'That's not what I'm suggesting,' Rebecca said quietly. 'Penny deserves the best care available and, on either side of the actual surgery, you are the person who can provide that.'

'And you are the person who can provide the best surgical care,' he responded. 'She deserves that, too.' He closed his eyes in a slow blink and then met her gaze again. 'So what is it that you *are* suggesting?'

'That we talk. Not here,' she added quickly. 'Somewhere more…' She cleared her throat. 'Somewhere else.'

Had she been going to suggest somewhere more private? Like the house they'd lived in with Gwen that Rebecca had refused to sell?

He couldn't do that. What if she still had all those pictures on the walls? That old basket with the toys in it, even?

'I'm going for a walk after work,' Rebecca said quietly. 'Through Regent's Park and over to Primrose Hill. It's a gorgeous day. Why don't you come with me?'

A walk. In a public place. Enough space that

nobody would be able to overhear anything that might be said and the ability to walk away if it proved impossible to find common ground without this horrible tension.

Except they had to find that common ground, didn't they, if they were going to work together?

If they couldn't, Thomas would have to add a failure to remain professional to the list of his other shortcomings and this one wouldn't be private—it would be fodder for gossip and damaging for both their careers.

And his career was all he had left now.

'Fine.' He nodded. 'Page me when you're done for the day. I'll be here.'

Out of one meeting and straight into another.

Rebecca only had time to duck into her office and grab a folder from her desk before heading down to the coffee shop on the ground floor where the committee members in charge of organising the Teddy Bears' Picnic would be waiting for her.

The countdown was on for the annual event

that Rebecca had been instrumental in setting up four years ago and this one promised to be the biggest and best yet.

The committee president, a mother of a child with cystic fibrosis who had received a double lung transplant six years ago, waved excitedly at Rebecca and she weaved her way through the busy café opposite the pharmacy on the ground floor.

'We had to start without you, I'm afraid.'

'No problem, Janice. I'm so sorry I'm late.' It seemed to be becoming the theme of her day today, but at least she didn't have anyone glaring at her. Janice was beaming, in fact.

'I've got *such* good news. Your suggestion to contact the president of the World Transplant Games Federation really paid off. We're going to have trouble choosing which inspirational speakers we want the most.'

'Oh? That's fantastic.' Rebecca smiled up at the young waitress taking orders. 'I'll have a flat white, please. And one of your gorgeous savoury muffins.' The way her day was shaping up, it was highly likely to be the only lunch she would get.

'We've got an offer from a man called Jeremy Gibson. He got a liver transplant when he was in his early thirties and had three young children. He's competed in the games for four years now and, last year, he led a sponsored hike in the Himalayas to raise awareness for organ donation and advertise how successful it can be.'

Rebecca nodded but she wasn't quite focused on this new meeting yet. The way Thomas had looked at her—after he'd asked if she wanted to call in a new cardiologist for Penny's case…

The tension had still been there. That undercurrent of anger that she knew had been caused by her telling him that he always ran away was still there. But there'd been something else, as well. A sadness that had made her want to walk around the edge of that table and simply put her arms around him.

To tell him how sorry she was.

For everything.

That was a bit of a shock, all by itself. She was over the breakup of her marriage.

She was over Thomas.

Who, in their right mind, would choose to be with someone who simply wasn't there when the going got too rough?

'And then there's Helena Adams,' Janice continued. 'A double lung recipient who's a champion skier and…' She consulted a notepad on the table in front of her. 'And Connor O'Brien—a young heart transplant recipient who ran in the London Marathon last year.'

'They all sound amazing,' Rebecca said.

'Maybe they could all come,' their treasurer suggested. 'They don't all have to speak. They could just mingle and join in some of the fun and chat to parents and kids. And the press, of course. We're going to get way more coverage this year, what with the threat to Paddington's already getting so much publicity.'

'We've got three television crews coming,' the secretary added. 'We're going international, apparently.' She fanned her face. 'This is all getting so much bigger than we ever thought it would.'

'Okay.' Janice's deep breath was audible. 'Let's get on with everything on the agenda. We've got a lot to get through. Has the bouncy castle been booked?'

'Yes. It's huge. And it's got turrets and everything. I've got a picture here…'

'Oh, it's perfect,' someone said. 'And how appropriate, given that Paddington's nickname is "the Castle"?'

An old redbrick Victorian building, Paddington Children's Hospital did indeed have its own turrets—the largest of which was a distinctive slate-roofed dome that loomed above the reception area of the main entrance.

'What's more important is to decide where it's going to go. I'm not sure the layout worked as well as it could last year and we've got so many extra things this time. The zoo has offered to organise and run pony rides.' Janice looked around the table. 'I know the London Zoo is one of our biggest sponsors and that's why we go over the road to Primrose Hill but is it going to be big enough? Do we need to consider a shift to part of Regent's Park?'

'I'm going to go there this evening,' Rebecca told them. 'I'll take the draft plan for the layout with me and walk it out but I think it'll be fine. We had tons of extra space last year and it was lovely to be on top of the hill and see everything that was going on. Some of the photos were fabulous, weren't they?'

She caught her lip between her teeth, her thoughts wandering again as the other committee members reminisced about last year's success. Should she have told Thomas the reason she was planning that walk in the park after work today?

No. If he'd known it had anything to do with the children and families of both donors and recipients of transplanted organs, he would have run a mile.

They really needed to talk if they were going to be able to work together and he didn't need to know the real reason she was there, did he? It was summer and the evenings were long. She could always stay later than him and sit on the top of the hill with the plan in her hands and make any notes she needed for changes.

It was important that they spent this time together. Before things got any more difficult between them.

And she was looking forward to it. Kind of. In a purely professional sense, of course. She'd feel better when she'd had the chance to apologise for that verbal attack. Thomas hadn't deserved that. She knew he was doing his best in the only way he knew how. That he had probably been doing that all along. It was just so sad that he couldn't see that he'd chosen such a wrong path.

That he, above everybody else, was suffering more because of it.

In retrospect, however, there was another reason why inviting Thomas to share this walk might have been a bad idea. It hadn't occurred to her at the time that a walk up Primrose Hill was an echo of their very first date.

Maybe he wouldn't remember. It wouldn't matter if he did. Just breathing the same air as Thomas was an echo of so very many things and, somehow, they had to find a way to deal with that.

CHAPTER THREE

THE WARMTH OF the summer's evening did not seem to be doing much to thaw the chill that surrounded Thomas and Rebecca like an air-conditioned bubble.

The virtual silence for the brisk walk to Regent's Park had been largely disguised by the sounds of the busy city streets but it became increasingly obvious as they followed a path into the vast stretch of green space.

'Thanks for agreeing to come,' Rebecca offered, finally.

'As you said, we need to find a way we can work together. Without letting our personal baggage interfere in any way with patient care.'

It sounded as though Thomas had rehearsed that little speech. Maybe it had been something he'd said to himself more than once today. Because he'd been arguing with himself about whether or not he could bear to spend any time with her?

Rebecca took a deep breath and did her best not to let it out as a sigh. He was here, walking beside her, so that was a good start. Maybe it was too soon to open the can of worms that was their 'personal baggage.' If Thomas could actually relax a fraction, it could make this a whole lot easier. And who wouldn't relax on a walk like this?

The boat lake beside them was a popular place to be on such a warm, sunny evening. It was crowded with boats—classic wooden rowing boats and the bright blue and yellow paddle boats. The grassy banks were dotted with the rugs and folding chairs of groups of families and friends who were preparing for a picnic meal. There were dogs chasing balls and children playing games on the shore of the lake.

And there were ducks.

Of course there were ducks. How many times had she and Thomas come here with Gwen on those precious days when she wasn't with her caregiver or at nursery school? They'd started bringing her here to feed the ducks way before she was old enough to walk or throw a crust of bread.

Not that she was about to remind Thomas of those times. Or admit that she still automatically put crusts of bread into a bag in the freezer until it was so full it would remind her that she never had the time or motivation to feed ducks any more. No one seeing them would ever guess at the kind of shared history they had. They would see the tall man with his briefcase in his hand and his companion with the strap of her laptop case over her shoulder and assume that they were work colleagues who happened to be sharing a walk home at the end of their day.

Exactly the space they were in, thanks to the boundaries that had been put firmly in place from the moment Thomas had set foot in Paddington's again.

Except that Thomas was smiling. Almost. He had his hand up to shield his eyes as he took in the scene of the boating activity on the lake and his lips were definitely not in a straight line.

His breath came out in an audible huff that could have been suppressed laughter.

'Nobody's swimming today,' he murmured.

It wasn't a lake that anybody swam in. Unless they were unfortunate enough to fall out of a boat, of course.

Like she had that day…

Good grief. She had deliberately avoided opening that can of worms labelled 'shared memories' but Thomas hadn't even hesitated.

Okay, it was funny in retrospect but it hadn't been at the time. Thomas had been inspired by the romantic image of a date that involved rowing his girlfriend around a pretty lake and Rebecca had been dressed for the occasion in a floaty summer dress and a wide-brimmed straw sunhat.

It had been a gloriously sunny day but there'd been a decent breeze. Enough to catch her hat and send it sailing away to float on the water. Thomas had done his best to row close enough for her to lean out of the boat and retrieve the hat but he hadn't been quite close enough. And she'd leaned just a little too far.

The water had been shallow enough to stand up in but she'd been completely soaked and the filmy dress had been clinging to her body and transparent enough to make her underwear obvious. The shock of the dunking had given way to helpless laughter and then to something very different when she'd seen the look in Thomas's eyes. Getting out of those wet clothes and into a hot bath hadn't been the real reason they couldn't get home fast enough.

And now, with Thomas pulling that memory out to share, Rebecca had the sensation that shutters had been lifted. There was a glint in his eyes that made her feel as if she'd stepped back in time.

As if everything they'd had together was still there—just waiting to have life breathed into it again.

It was the last thing Rebecca had expected to feel. It was too much. It wasn't what she wanted. She didn't want to go anywhere near that kind of space in her head or her heart and that made it…what…terrifying?

She had to break that eye contact. To push that memory back where it belonged—firmly in the past.

'Nobody sensible would,' she heard herself saying. 'But we all make mistakes, don't we?'

She hadn't looked away fast enough to miss the way that glint in his eyes got extinguished and her words hung in the air as they walked on, taking on a whole new meaning. That the mistake that had been made encompassed their whole relationship?

The soft evening air began to feel increasingly thick with the growing tension. This was her fault, Rebecca realised. She'd had the opportunity to break the ice and make things far more comfortable between them and she'd ruined it because she'd backed off so decisively. Maybe it was up to her to find another way to defuse the tension. At least she was no stranger to tackling difficult subjects with her patients and their families.

She had learned it was best to start in a safe place and not to jump in the deep end as Thomas had—perhaps—inadvertently done.

'I did that consult you requested on your new patient this afternoon. Tegan Mitchell? The thirteen-year-old with aortic stenosis?'

'Ah…good.' There was a note of relief in his voice as he responded to stepping onto safe, professional ground. 'What did you think?'

'Classic presentation. Even my junior house surgeon could hear the ejection click after the first heart sound and the ejection murmur. It was the first time she'd come across an example of how the murmur increases with squatting and decreases with standing. She's got some impressive oedema in her legs and feet, too.' Rebecca's lips curled into a small smile as she glanced up at Thomas. 'Tegan, that is, not my house surgeon—*her* legs are fine.'

Thomas didn't smile at her tongue-in-cheek clarification. 'I've got Tegan booked for an echo tomorrow morning. We've started medication to get her heart failure under control but I think she's a good candidate for valve replacement surgery, yes?'

That tension hadn't been defused enough to allow for a joke, obviously. Rebecca nodded. 'Absolutely.'

He didn't see her nod because he had turned his head as the path forked.

'Do you want to go through Queen Mary's Garden?'

'Why not? It'll be gorgeous with the roses in full bloom.'

Thomas took the lead through the ornate gates and chose a path between gardens with immaculately trimmed hedges surrounding waves of colour. Rebecca inhaled the heady scent of old-fashioned roses but Thomas didn't seem at all distracted by the beauty around them.

'How's your theatre list looking for later this week?'

'Not too bad but it can always go pear-shaped at a moment's notice if a transplant organ becomes available—especially if I have to fly somewhere for the retrieval. I've got two cystic fibrosis kids on the ward now who are desperate for new lungs and I can get called in for other cases, too. I started my transplant training with kidneys and livers, way back. I still love helping with those surgeries when I'm needed.'

'Way back? Five years isn't so long ago.'

'Mmm.' The sound was neutral. Five years could seem like for ever, couldn't it?

As if to push her thoughts where they probably shouldn't really go, a young couple passed them on the wide path. The woman was pushing an empty stroller. The man had a safe grip on the legs of the small child on his shoulders who was happily keeping his balance with fistfuls of his father's hair.

Five years ago she and Thomas would have looked more like this couple than a pair of colleagues. They had been happily married with an adorable three-year-old daughter. They were both juggling careers and parenthood and thriving on their lifestyle even though it frequently bordered on chaotic.

They hadn't intended to have a child so soon,

of course, but the surprise of her pregnancy when Rebecca was studying for her finals in medical school had quickly morphed into joy. It had been meant to happen—just like they'd been meant to meet and fall in love so completely. They'd announced the pregnancy to the gathering of friends and family who'd come together to celebrate their low-key wedding and brushed off any concerns about how they would manage those busy early years of hospital training with a baby in their lives.

'We'll cope,' they had both repeated with absolute confidence. *'We've got each other.'*

And they *had* coped. They had known exactly what specialties they had set their hearts on and Rebecca was chasing her dream of being a cardiothoracic surgeon with as much passion as Thomas put into his postgraduate studies in paediatric cardiology. The firsthand experience of being parents only confirmed what they also already knew—that they were destined to always work with children.

So yes, right now, five years was a lifetime ago.

And it had been a long time since Thomas had turned his back on the specialty he'd worked so hard to get into.

'How are you finding being back at Paddington's?' she heard herself asking.

The look she received was almost bewildered.

'I mean, working with children again,' she added hurriedly. 'It must be very different to what you were doing up north...' Oh, help! This wasn't exactly staying on safe ground to get a conversation going, was it?

'It was...a big change...' It sounded as though Thomas was treading carefully—unsure of how much he wanted to say. 'I knew it wasn't going to be easy...'

Wow.

The step he'd voluntarily taken onto personal ground was as unexpected as him referring, however obliquely, to that date when she'd fallen out of the boat. Rebecca had no idea what to say in response. Should she offer sympathy which might immediately lead the conversation into the reasons why it hadn't been easy? To tell him how hard it had been for her, too—to be around children in those grief-stricken months after losing Gwen?

Even now, it could stir the threat of tears that had always been barely below the surface of her existence back then. How often did she have to fight for control? Whenever she heard the cry of a child and the soothing sound of a mother offering comfort. Or she saw the smile of a toddler or heard the delicious sound of a baby giggling. And the hardest thing of all was when she was holding one of her tiny patients herself. Or when a small child held their arms up, expecting the cuddle she would never refuse.

No. She wasn't ready to talk about that. And it would be the last thing Thomas would want to hear about. He had only agreed to this time together in order to clear the air enough for them to be able to work together. Perhaps what was really needed was a way to put more effective boundaries around the past so that they could both move on with their lives.

'No,' she finally said quietly. 'But everybody's delighted that you've come back.'

There was a moment's silence. Was he wondering if she was including herself in that 'everybody'?

'And you're here at such an important time for Paddington's,' Rebecca added quickly. 'You arrived right at the point where we all thought it was the end and then, thanks to the huge drama of that fire at Westbourne Grove Primary School, the media got on board and things started to turn around.'

'Yeah… I did think I might be accepting a permanent job at a hospital that wasn't going to be around much longer. Seemed a bit crazy at the time.'

'But now it looks like it's going to be all right. I know it's not really official yet but it sounds like it's going to be signed and sealed any day now. Are you going to the party at the Frog and Peach on Friday?'

Thomas shrugged. 'I'll have to see how the day goes.'

'Me, too. I often seem to be pretty late getting away once I've caught up on paperwork and things.'

'Same.'

Did they both work such long hours because there was nothing to make them rush home? Rebecca hadn't heard the slightest whisper of gossip that there might be someone else in Thomas's life now. She didn't even know where he was living, in fact.

'I hope this isn't taking you too far out of your way,' she said politely. 'Or keeping you from something you'd rather be doing on a nice summer's evening.'

'It's not a problem,' Thomas said. 'And it's not far to get home. I've got an apartment in South Hampstead.' He cleared his throat. 'And you? You still in Primrose Hill?'

'Mmm.' It was another tricky subject. Buying the basement flat in such a good area had been a huge step in their lives together and they couldn't have done it without the windfall of the legacy from Rebecca's grandfather. Thomas had refused to accept any of that money in the divorce settlement so he'd walked away with almost nothing.

'Keep it,' he'd said. *'Keep everything. I don't want any reminders.'*

Which reminders had been on the top of that list?

The night they'd taken possession and had a picnic on the bare floor of the living area with fish and chips and a bottle of champagne? Had either of them even noticed the discomfort of the wooden boards when they'd made love as the final celebration of getting the keys to their first home?

They'd decided later that that had been the night Gwen had been conceived and that had been as perfect as everything else in their charmed existence.

A sideways glance gave her a moment of eye contact with Thomas and she saw the flash of surprise in his face. Oh, help! Had he seen what she'd been thinking about just then? The way she'd known he'd been remembering how she'd looked with that dress plastered so revealingly to her body after her dunking in the lake?

It was too easy to read too much into those glances. There were too many memories. And yes, some of them were the best moments of her life but they had been buried under far more overwhelming ones.

Maybe the biggest reminders of sharing that house were the ones that included Gwen after her birth? Walking round and round that small space, trying to persuade their tiny human to go to sleep. A floor that was an obstacle course because it was covered with toys. The sound of a little girl's laughter that echoed between the polished floorboards and the high ceilings…

She'd had to live with those reminders and, for the longest time, tears had done little to wash away the pain they caused. But gradually—so slowly Rebecca had barely noticed it happening—something had changed and sometimes there was comfort to be found in them.

Gwen's room might have become an office but occasionally, when Rebecca was working there late at night, she would remember going in just to watch Gwen sleep for a moment. She would take that warm, fuzzy miracle of loving and being loved so much and wrap it around herself like the softest blanket imaginable. Sometimes, Thomas would come with her and they'd stand there hand in hand and the blanket would be wrapped around them both. And it would still be around them when they went to sit on the big, old couch that dominated the small living room. Or it would be an extra layer on the antique brass bed that was big enough to almost touch both sides of their bedroom.

The couch was still there.

And the bed.

Were the memories that lingered even after all this time something else that Thomas had been so desperate to get away from?

Rebecca had chosen to stay. To live with those memories.

To cope with the loneliness of losing all that love…

CHAPTER FOUR

THEY'D BEEN WALKING in silence for a long time, now.

Thomas stole a sideways glance at Rebecca. What was she thinking about?

What had they been talking about?

Oh, yeah, where they were living.

She was still in that house they'd chosen together. Had he imagined it or did she still remember the way they'd celebrated when they'd picked up the keys and had finally been alone together in their first, real home? The idea that he'd caught a glimpse of that memory in her eyes when their gazes had touched might have been purely projection but even if she had forgotten that particular night, there was no way she could escape all the other memories.

He couldn't begin to imagine being able to

have done that himself. How could you escape from memories that made you feel as if your heart was being ripped out of your chest when they were all around you? When even the walls had soaked up the sounds of a newborn baby's cry and an infant's laughter and the first words of a toddler?

It was just as incomprehensible as choosing to take your career into an area that held memories that were still too raw to go near. To actually take a child into an operating theatre to harvest organs when you knew the kind of grief the parents were experiencing had to mean you could shut yourself away completely.

To stop caring to the extent that it was possible to think of those organs as 'spare parts'?

Thomas could feel the muscles in his jaw tensing so much they made his teeth ache.

No wonder their marriage had failed.

Maybe they'd never really understood each other.

Their route had taken them right through Regent's Park now and they were walking past the perimeter of London Zoo. A screech of some excited animal could be heard—an orangutan, perhaps? Thomas hadn't been near a zoo for five years and he wasn't comfortable being this close. There were memories everywhere, here. A lazy Sunday afternoon, pushing Gwen's stroller down the paths and stopping to try and capture her expressions when she saw the animals and birds. The penguins had been her absolute favourite and she'd shrieked with laughter every time they waddled close to the fence.

They'd bought a stuffed toy penguin in the zoo shop that had been almost as big as she was but it had to be tucked into bed with her that night. And she'd fallen asleep, still smiling...

Thomas waited for the jolt of pain that always came with memories like that. He could feel his muscles tense and his face scrunch into a scowl, as if that would somehow protect him.

Rebecca seemed oblivious. She was heading for the other side of Prince Albert Road, clearly intent on getting to Primrose Hill and that was good. The further away from the zoo they got, the better. He wouldn't have to mentally swat away more memories.

Like the way Rebecca's face would light up with pleasure when they watched the otters which were *her* absolute favourite.

Or that photograph that someone had offered to take of them as a family, beside the huge, bronze statue of the gorilla just inside the entrance to the zoo. He'd been holding Gwen with one arm and had his other arm around Rebecca. Their heads had both been level with his shoulders and he must have said something funny, because they'd both looked up at him as the photo was taken and they were all grinning from ear to ear.

Looking so happy…

His scowl deepened as they reached the entrance to Primrose Hill Park because now they were going past the children's playground.

For a split second, his gaze caught Rebecca's as they glanced at each other at precisely the same moment. He knew they were both thinking the same thing—that the last time they'd been to this playground, they'd been with their daughter.

They'd probably both looked away from each other in the same moment, as well.

There were more memories, here. More jolts of pain to be expected.

Except...that first one hadn't arrived yet.

That was weird. How could he actually have such a clear picture in his head of something like Gwen being tucked up with her toy penguin and not feel the same crippling blast of loss that he'd had the last time his brain had summoned something like that from that private databank of images?

As if he needed to prod the wound to check whether it was possible that it had miraculously started healing, Thomas let himself think about it again. He could see Gwen's dark curls against the pale pillowcase, her cheek pressed against the fluff of the penguin. He could see the sweep of her dark lashes become still as sleep claimed her and he could see the dimples that came with even the smallest smile.

And yes, he could feel the pang of loss and a wash of sadness but it wasn't really pain. He could—almost—feel his own lips trying to curl up at the corners.

Instead of relief, this awareness that something had changed brought something far less pleasant with it.

Guilt?

Was he somehow failing Gwen by being less traumatised at being reminded of her loss?

Maybe grappling with a sense of failure was familiar enough to be preferable to something strange and new.

He'd been over this ground often enough in the past few years. How he'd failed Gwen as a father because he hadn't been able to keep her safe.

How he'd failed Rebecca as a husband because he hadn't been able to keep their marriage alive.

But how could it have worked when they were such different people? People who had never really understood each other?

'Do you mind if we stop for a moment?'

'Not getting puffed, are you? We're not even at the top of the hill.' Unbidden, another memory ambushed him. 'I seem to remember you ran up here the last time we did this. Faster than I managed.'

Rebecca's face went very still.

She hadn't forgotten that moment in time, had she?

Their very first date. A walk in the park and the decision to get to the top of the hill to admire the view.

'Race you!'

'Last one there is a rotten egg!'

She'd won that race but she'd had to throw herself onto the grass to try and catch her breath. And Thomas had lain down beside her and neither of them had bothered to look at anything more than each other between those lingering kisses. The walk down the hill had been much, much slower. Holding hands and exchanging glances so frequently, as if they needed to confirm that they were both feeling the same way—that they'd found a hand to hold that would get them through the rest of their lives...

Oh, man, this walk together really hadn't been a very good idea, had it? It was doing his head in.

This was all so hard and exactly what he'd been determined to avoid when he'd chosen to come back to Paddington's.

But Rebecca was staring down the hill, her face still expressionless, seemingly focused on something that had nothing to do with any memories of their first date.

'I just need to check something.'

'What?'

'Um…' Rebecca's eyes were narrowed against the glare of the sun as she looked down the slope. 'We need a flat area for both the pony rides and the bouncy castle…'

Thomas blinked. 'You've lost me.'

'I'm on the organising committee for a big picnic that's happening soon. It's our fourth year and it's going to get a lot more publicity this year because of Paddington's being in the spotlight with the threatened closure. We need to make sure there are no glitches, so I'm checking out the plan.'

Something like a chill ran down Thomas's spine.

'I saw the poster in the relatives' room. It's for transplant patients, yes?' He could hear the chill in his tone. He didn't want to start talking about any of this. Except that this was the reason they couldn't work well together, wasn't it? And that was why they were here now.

They *had* to talk about it.

'Not just the patients. It's to celebrate everything that's good about organ donation in the hope of getting people more aware and making it easier to talk about.' Rebecca's tone was cautious enough to reveal that she, too, recognised they were approaching the real point of this time together. 'It's for the patients and their families, of course, but also for all the people who devote their working lives to making the success stories happen. And…and it's for the people on the other side, too. Some people have contact with the recipients of their child's organs and…and even if they don't, it's a day where they can celebrate the gift of life they were able to provide.'

Julia had said something about a parent like that but it was in the 'unthinkable' basket for

Thomas. To see another child that was having fun at some amazing picnic with pony rides and a bouncy castle because they had a part of *his* daughter?

The chill in his spine held an edge of horror now.

Did *Rebecca* know a child like that?

He wasn't going to ask. *He* didn't want to know.

Refreshing that smouldering pile that was the anger that had been ignited last week was a preferable route to feeling either so disturbed by unexpected memories or guilty about things he had or hadn't done in the past.

'Yes,' he heard himself saying aloud. 'I guess you need to drum up a good supply of those *spare* parts.'

The silence that fell between them was like a solid wall.

Impenetrable.

It stretched out for long enough to take a slow breath. And then another.

They weren't even looking at each other. They could have been on separate planets.

And then Rebecca spoke.

'I should never have said that. I'm sorry. It was completely unprofessional. And…and it was cruel.'

'I couldn't agree more.'

'It's not what I believe,' she said softly. '*You* know that, Tom.'

It was the first time she'd called him Tom since he'd come back and it touched a place that had been very safely walled off.

Or maybe it was that assumption that he knew her well enough to know that she would never think like that.

And, deep down, he had known that, hadn't he? It had just been so much easier to think otherwise. To be angry.

'So, why did you say it, then?'

'You've been so distant ever since you came back. So cut off. I don't even recognise you any more.' There was a hitch in Rebecca's voice that went straight to that place that calling him 'Tom' had accessed. 'I guess I wanted to know if the man I married still exists.'

His words were a little less of a snap this time. 'I haven't changed.'

'Yes, you have.' He could feel Rebecca looking at him but he didn't turn his head. 'Something like what we went through changes everyone. But you...you disappeared. You just...ran away.'

There was that accusation again. That he was a coward.

The reminder of how little she understood came with a wave of weariness. Thomas wanted this over with. He wanted to put this all behind them effectively enough to be able to work together.

He wanted...peace.

So he took another deep breath and he turned his head to meet Rebecca's gaze.

'Everyone processes grief differently. You should know as well as anybody that it's not a good idea to make assumptions.'

'But that's the problem,' Rebecca whispered. 'It always was.'

'What?'

'That you *didn't* process it. You shut yourself

away. Emotionally and then physically. You left me. You left Paddington's.'

That was unfair.

'I didn't *leave* you. It was *you* who asked for the divorce.'

'You did leave me.' Rebecca's eyes were bright enough to suggest gathering tears. 'You started walking away the day Gwen died and I felt more and more alone until the idea of staying in our marriage was worse than escaping.'

Thomas was silent. He had a horrible feeling that those words were going to haunt him from now on and that they would be harder to deal with than an accusation of cowardice.

'You don't even want to talk to me any more. You've been here for months now and you've avoided anything that doesn't have something to do with a patient. You can't even ask whether I've had a good day, let alone talk about something like the Teddy Bears' Picnic. And...' Rebecca was clearly struggling to hold back her tears now. She sniffed inelegantly. 'And you never smile. And you call me Rebecca. Or Dr Scott. Like I'm…a complete stranger.'

Thomas closed his eyes for a moment. It was true. He'd created as much distance as he could to try and make their first meeting easier and he'd kept it up. For months…

'I… I'm sorry.'

Rebecca nodded. She sniffed again and then scrubbed at her nose with the back of her hand.

'Excuse me. I don't have a hanky,' she said.

'Neither do I.' Thomas wished he did. Offering one could have been an olive branch. And they needed an olive branch.

'You're right,' he said slowly. 'I have been distant. I knew it was going to be hard working with children again. I thought I'd be making it a whole lot harder if I spent time with you, as well.'

'You don't have to spend time with me to be friendly. Just a smile would do. Or saying something friendly that made me feel like a person and not just a surgical consult.'

Thomas nodded. 'I could do that. Something like "Have you had a good day?"'

It was Rebecca's turn to nod. But then her breath escaped in a huff of sound that was more like a sob. 'Actually, I've had a horrible day. Ever since you glared at me for being late for the meeting this morning and everybody was reminded of how much you hate working with me.'

'I don't hate working with you. You're the best surgeon I have available. I think…your skills are amazing.'

'But you'd rather it was someone else with my skills.'

'You probably found it easier to work with the cardiologist I replaced.'

She shook her head this time. 'Not professionally. You're the best, too.'

'But personally,' Thomas persisted, 'you don't find it any easier than I do.'

'Only because you hate me.'

Thomas sighed. 'Oh, Becca… I could never *hate* you.'

The short version of her name had slipped out, as Thomas turned to look at her directly, so he could see the effect it had. Her face became very

CHAPTER FIVE

THOMAS WOLFE WASN'T the only person in the gallery to watch this particular surgery.

Rosie Hobbes was sitting beside him, alternatively watching the screen that gave a close-up view of what was largely obscured by the gowned and masked figures below and leaning forward to watch the whole team at work.

'I've never seen the insertion of a VAD before.'

'No. It's not common. Especially in children.'

'Do you think it'll work?'

'It will certainly buy us some time. The only thing that could guarantee more time is a transplant. This is a bridge which should give her a much better quality of life while we're waiting.'

Rosie was looking down into the theatre again. At the small chest now open and so vulnerable.

'Life's so unfair sometimes, isn't it?' she murmured.

'Mmm.' Thomas couldn't argue with that. He had firsthand experience of exactly how unfair life could be. So did the surgeon he was watching so intently.

The last time he had watched Rebecca operate had, ironically, been on this same patient, when Penny had been only about six months old.

Life wasn't only unfair, it had patterns to it. Circles. Or were they spirals? A kind of pathway, anyway, that could take you back to places you'd been before. Places where memories could be looked at through a lens that changed with increased distance or wisdom.

Did you choose to follow those pathways with the familiar signposts, Thomas wondered. Or were they somehow set in place by fate and always there, waiting for you to step back onto them? Spirals could go either way, couldn't they? They could go downwards into tight loops that sucked you into a place you didn't want to be.

Or they could lift you higher into loops so wide that the possibilities were no more than promises.

He was, very unexpectedly, back on one of his life pathways. Ever since that walk with Rebecca the other day when they'd reached some kind of truce and sealed it with that hug.

Or maybe he'd stepped back onto that path the moment he'd agreed to come back to Paddington's.

It still felt weird.

The way the memories had begun to rush at him from every direction but without the pain he would have expected.

He could think of Gwen and find himself ready to smile.

He could remember Rebecca falling out of that boat and how unbelievably sexy she'd looked in that wet dress...

He had even found himself reliving that hug on the top of Primrose Hill and how it had reminded him—again—of their very first date.

'We're ready to go on bypass.' Rebecca's voice was calm and clear through the speaker system.

'And the pocket for the pump is all set. How's the pump preparation looking?'

The surgeon working on the back table to prepare the device looked up and nodded. 'Ready when you are.'

'Stand by.' Rebecca and her registrar started the task of getting Penny onto bypass. Despite her obvious focus, she kept her audience involved. 'Because we know that this surgery is a bridge to transplant, I'm being careful to leave space for re-cannulation at the aortic cannulation site.'

It took long minutes to get Penny onto bypass and to the point where the heart was stopped. Her life now depended on the oxygen being circulated by the cardiopulmonary bypass machine. It was a procedure that was common and relatively safe these days but it still gave Thomas a sense of wonder at what medicine was able to achieve, along with a dollop of pride that he was able to be a part of this astonishing world.

He was proud of Rebecca, too. He had been perfectly sincere when he'd told her that she was the best surgeon he had available and that her skills were amazing, but he hadn't realised how much better she had become in the last few years. So confident but, at the same time, so exquisitely careful of every tiny detail. His gaze was fixed on the screen again as she inserted a suture.

'This marks the site of the core,' she said, for the benefit of the observers. 'I've used the left anterior descending artery to identify the intra-ventricular groove. We're going to core anteriorly due to the small size of the left ventricle.'

We. It was Rebecca who was doing the actual task but she'd never shown any sign of developing the ego that some surgeons were famous for. She'd always seen herself as part of a team.

And now Thomas felt like he was part of that team, too. As difficult as it had been to step onto personal ground during that walk, they had found a space just within the perimeter that was apparently going to make it possible to work together without the awful tension of the last months.

Maybe it would even allow them to become friends one day.

It had also given him rather a lot to think about.

The quiet conversations between the surgeons, nursing staff and technicians below were only catching the surface layer of his attention as his thoughts drifted back to what was becoming a familiar route.

He'd known that her heartfelt words would haunt him.

I felt more and more alone...

He'd felt alone, too. They might have been walking the same path back then, in those dark days, but they had been nowhere near each other and the distance had only increased.

Looking back, he could see that it had been Rebecca who'd made the effort to reach out time and time again.

'I've kept some dinner for you. It's in the oven.'
'I'm not hungry.'

The bed, where they would lie side by side, should have made them feel less alone but those sleepless hours had been the worst. The slightest contact with her skin would make him flinch and move away.

'It's been a long day. I'm tired.'

But he'd *been* there. He hadn't been running away. He'd been desperately sad. He'd needed more time to try and put the shattered pieces of his life back together and it was something that Rebecca couldn't help with. Not just because she was fighting her own battle but because she was so much a piece of what had been shattered.

His family.

The family that he had failed to protect.

She'd been right to accuse him of being distant ever since he'd returned to Paddington's. Was she also right that he'd coped with his grief by initiating that distance all those years ago? Had he been the one to push them so far apart that there had been no hope of connecting enough to help each other?

How could he have let that happen to the person who'd been his whole world until Gwen had arrived? The only woman he would ever love like that…

'Look at that,' Rosie whispered beside him. 'That's the inflow cannula going in and getting secured to the sewing ring. Dr Scott's incredibly neat, isn't she?'

Rebecca's size had often led people to make incorrect assumptions about her abilities but having such small hands with those long, delicate fingers was a bonus for a surgeon who often had to work on tiny patients. Being so much shorter than he was had always seemed another bonus because it made it easier for children to be drawn to her. At six foot one, Thomas towered over his small patients. And when was the last time he had crouched down to talk to one of them? Had he forgotten the difference that could make in his years of working only with adults?

Maybe he'd forgotten how tall he was, along with ignoring so many other personal things that only intruded on his focus on his work.

Hugging Rebecca on Primrose Hill had made him acutely aware of his height because of the way her head only reached his shoulder. Not that that had ever been a bad thing. As if it was a step from a well-remembered dance, she had turned her head so that it fitted perfectly into the natural hollow beneath his collarbone. It probably wasn't such a good thing that holding her that close had also reminded him of how soft her curves were...

With an effort, Thomas refocused on what he'd come here to watch. Brooding about how much he had failed Rebecca to leave her feeling so unbearably alone that she'd had to escape her marriage was not only inappropriate, it wasn't going to help anyone. The past was simply that—the past. They could only move forward and now they seemed to have found a way to do that.

At least he'd been the one to reach out this time.

To offer that hug that was a physical connection on top of an emotional one.

And it had felt good.

More than good.

As if there was a promise in the air he was breathing now.

The promise of finding peace?

She knew he was watching her.

Not that she'd looked directly up at the gallery

at any point but she'd caught movement from the corner of her eye as she'd entered the theatre—her arms crossed in front of her, keeping her scrubbed and gloved hands safe from contact with anything—and she'd known it was Thomas, simply from the impression of height and that measured kind of movement he had these days.

Rebecca wasn't about to let anything disturb her focus. She did allow herself a heartbeat of pleasure that he was there but the only other irrelevant thought that escaped that part of her brain before she closed it down was that the last time Thomas had been observing her work had been during the second cardiac surgery that Penelope Craig had had, when she was still so tiny—only a few months old.

Or maybe the thought wasn't completely irrelevant. The surgery had been a success that time. She was going to do her utmost to make sure it was this time, too.

Finally, it was time to find out. The ventricular assist device had been meticulously stitched into position and Penny had been weaned off the cardiopulmonary bypass.

'We'll start the device at the lowest setting and keep the aortic clamp on to get rid of the last of the air.' Rebecca turned to one of the Theatre technicians. 'I'll need the transoesophageal echo soon, so I can check the final position in the chest without the retractors.'

She took plenty of time to gradually increase the flow of the device while the heart's function and pressures were closely monitored.

'We may not decide on final settings for a few days,' she said, for the benefit of everyone watching. 'Some people leave the chest open for a day to allow for stabilisation but I would only do that if I was concerned about something like ongoing bleeding. This is looking great, so I'll be happy to close. Let's get these cannulas removed and some chest drains in.'

There was movement again in the gallery and Rebecca glanced up to see that some people were leaving now that the procedure was all but over and it had clearly been successful. Thomas was still there, however. He acknowledged her glance with a nod and the hint of a smile.

A smile…

Things had certainly changed in the last few days.

That hug on Primrose Hill had been a turning point. A starting point, perhaps, of a new relationship. One of colleagues who could work together without causing discomfort to themselves and those around them.

Maybe it could even be the start of a friendship?

Rebecca turned back to coach her registrar through the placement of the chest drains. She had to admit that the idea of being friends with Thomas might be pushing things and getting closer than colleagues might not be a good idea, anyway. It had messed with her head more than a little, that hug. Especially coming in the wake of so many memories that had been undisturbed for so long. Not that she'd ever forgotten how it had felt to be held in his arms with her head nestled in that hollow beneath his shoulder but she'd never expected to actually feel it again.

But, like the memories that they'd shared, that hug had stirred up feelings that might be far better left alone.

Like how much she had missed Thomas in her life.

How much she *still* missed him…

No. She missed having a partner but Thomas would never be that man, again. You couldn't rewrite history and too much damage had been done.

Minutes ticked past to add another hour to the long stint in Theatre but Rebecca wasn't about to leave her small patient under the complete care of others. Even when the surgery was completely finished and she had stripped off her gloves and mask and hat to dispose of them in the rubbish, she stayed in the room, keeping a close watch on all the monitors as the team tidied up around Penny and prepared her for the transfer to Recovery. And then she went with them, still watching for any change in pressures or heart rhythm.

It was no surprise that Thomas arrived by her side almost immediately.

'She's stable,' Rebecca told him. 'It's looking good.'

He was scanning the bank of monitors himself. 'You did a fantastic job,' he said quietly. 'Julia and Peter are waiting in the relatives' room. Do you want to come with me to tell them the good news?'

'Of course.' She stayed a moment longer, however, moving to the head of the bed. She put her forefinger against her lips and then reached down to touch Penny's cheek gently. 'Be back soon, pet. Sleep tight.'

Sleep tight, don't let the bedbugs bite...

Had Thomas remembered the final goodnight she had always given Gwen? That soft touch that transferred a kiss and the whisper of an old rhyme that was irrelevant except that it was remembered from her own childhood.

When had it become something she had started to do with her youngest patients?

She couldn't remember. Somewhere in the last

few years, it had just become one of those automatic, preferably private things. Like a good luck charm? No. She was too much of a scientist for something like that. It was because she worked with children and you couldn't help connecting with them at a level that was never appropriate or possible with adults.

And maybe it was because she knew, better than most, how precious these little lives were.

If Thomas remembered, he didn't show any sign of it. He was still looking at the monitors, in fact, rather than the small person attached to them. Rebecca's heart sank a little as she followed him from the Recovery area. They might have made a breakthrough in their own relationship but was Thomas ever going to step any closer to his patients? Allow himself enough of an emotional connection to share the joy that came with success?

He certainly had a smile for Penny's parents.

'I'll let Rebecca tell you how well the surgery went but it was all I could have hoped for. You'll be able to go in and see her very soon.'

Julia burst into tears. Peter put his arms around her and ignored the tears rolling down his own cheeks.

'She'll have to go to intensive care after this, won't she?'

'Yes. But probably not for long. It's amazing how quickly children can bounce back from even open heart surgery.'

'And she's going to be better?' Julia lifted her head from her husband's chest. 'She won't need the wheelchair or to be on oxygen all the time?'

'That's what I expect.' Thomas nodded. He smiled again but the glance at his watch told Rebecca that he was already preparing to move on to his next patient. Stepping back from this emotional encounter with his patient's parents?

Perhaps he wasn't ready for the kind of connection that would allow him to share their intense relief with its glimmers of joy that would become hope. And she could understand that. If you were distant enough not to buy in to the joy, it meant that you were protected from the pain when things didn't go well. With many of the cases doctors like she and Thomas had in their care, the long term outlook wasn't good, so that pain was inevitable. Rebecca had learned to deal with it. To remind herself that it was worth it because of the heavier balance of the joy.

Thomas had chosen to step back.

To run away…

But he had come back. Surely being willing to work with children again was a sign that something big had changed. And there'd been moments during that walk when she could believe that the man she'd married really did still exist somewhere behind those barriers.

Baby steps…

Like the fact that he could smile at her again.

It wasn't as if the distance he kept made the care he provided any less thorough. He went above and beyond what most doctors did which was why it was, again, no surprise to find him in the intensive care unit late that evening, when Rebecca went back for a final check on Penny.

'I met Julia by the elevator. She's finally gone to get something to eat in the cafeteria and then she's coming back to stay the night with Penny.'

Thomas nodded. 'Are you still happy to lighten the sedation level as early as tomorrow morning?'

'Yes. She's been stable ever since the surgery. The VAD is working perfectly. We'll keep the pain control up, of course, but I wouldn't be surprised if she wakes up and wants to get out of bed and put her tutu on. Like Sapphire, there.'

Thomas glanced at the end of the bed where the sparkly blue, soft toy bear that Julia had bought as Penny's post-surgery gift was waiting for her to see as soon as she woke up. But he wasn't smiling. Did he know how desperately Penny wanted to be a ballerina? Did it matter?

'It's very late,' she added. 'What are you still doing at work?'

Had his career become his whole life, the way hers had?

Did he not have someone to go home to?

The thought had occurred to her before, but she'd never heard any hint of what Thomas's life outside the hospital contained these days. It had been five years. It shouldn't be surprising if he did have someone else in his life by now but Rebecca knew how much of a shock it would be.

She wasn't ready to find out.

'It is late,' he agreed. 'I was catching up on some work. Trying to decide whether or not to go to that thing at the pub over the road.'

'Oh, the Frog and Peach. I'd completely forgotten about the celebration drinks.' Rebecca looked at her watch. 'It's only ten p.m. The party should be only just getting going.'

How good would it be if she and Thomas could go to a work function together? To have a drink with their colleagues and make it obvious that they'd found a way to work together again?

'Saving Paddington's is definitely something to celebrate,' she said, looking up to catch his gaze. 'Shall we pop in? Just for a quick drink?'

He hesitated and she could almost see him following the same train of thought she'd just had.

'Sure,' he said. 'Why not? Give me a few minutes to sort what I've left on my desk and I'll meet you in Reception.'

CHAPTER SIX

WEIRDLY, THERE WAS almost nobody from Paddington's still at the Frog and Peach by the time Rebecca and Thomas arrived.

There were plenty of people, and an enthusiastic game of darts going on in one corner, but the only two remaining staff members were Matt McGrory, the burns specialist at Paddington's, and Alistair North, a paediatric neurosurgeon. They were standing at the bar, their glasses almost empty.

'Where is everybody?' Rebecca asked. 'What kind of party is this?'

'We started early,' Matt said. 'On the dot of six p.m. Some people are working tomorrow and others had families to get home to.'

'I was sure Quinn would be here. She's been so involved in the campaign to save the hospital.'

'Oh, she was.' Matt's smile reflected the kind of glow that only newfound love could bring. 'Simon's babysitter could only stay till ten, so she had to go home.'

'How *is* Simon?' Like many of the staff members at Paddington's, Rebecca's heart had been caught by the case of five-year-old Simon, who was Quinn's first foster child, when he'd been badly burned in the fire at Westbourne Grove Primary School.

But Matt was still smiling. 'He's doing great. The scars on his face are looking brilliant thanks to the wonders of spray-on skin. His arm will take a bit more work but the best thing is that his self-confidence seems to be growing by the day.'

'Maybe it's because you and Quinn are together?' Alistair suggested. 'Giving him a real family?'

'I'd like to take the credit but I reckon Maisie has to take most of it.'

'Who's Maisie?' Thomas asked.

'She's a rescue dog we rehomed. Gorgeous collie-cross. Simon adores her, and it's helping in ways we never expected. Like when we went to the park the other day. These kids about Simon's age came over and wanted to pat his dog and help throw the ball for her and I swear they didn't even notice his scars.'

'Oh, that's brilliant,' Rebecca said.

'Claire was here to start with, too,' Alistair said. 'It was the perfect opportunity to share the news that we've decided to stay in London.'

'That's great news,' Thomas said.

'She was looking forward to catching up with you,' Alistair said to Rebecca, 'but she's getting tired pretty easily these days so she went at the same time as Quinn.'

'I'm not surprised she's tired.' Rebecca smiled. 'Didn't I hear a rumour that you've got twins on the way?'

'Yes.' Alistair had the same kind of glow that Matt did. 'Not sure how that news got leaked so fast. It's very early days so we're being careful.'

Rebecca felt a pang of something poignant. She remembered what it was like to be so in love. To be so sure that you'd found the person you wanted to spend the rest of your life with. To be expecting a first baby...

Hopefully, these new couples within the ranks of their colleagues would have the happy-ever-after that she and Thomas had missed out on.

'I'll have to catch up with them both some other time,' she said. 'I wanted to tell Quinn what a great job she did. She put a lot of effort into that committee.'

'I'll tell her you noticed,' Matt said. 'She's over the moon about the result, that's for sure.' His smile broadened. 'I believe she's now on a new committee that's going to be organising the official celebration bash.'

Rebecca laughed. 'That sounds like Quinn. Any word on what sort of party it's going to be?'

'Black tie, from what I've heard. A big dinner with lots of speeches.'

'I'll look forward to it.'

'Me, too,' Alistair said. 'In the meantime, can I buy you guys a drink? It's good to see you out and about for once, Thomas.'

'Ah...' Thomas's gaze slid sideways. Towards

the door? Was he thinking that the fact that this wasn't really a work function any more was a good reason to bail?

'I'll have a white wine,' Rebecca said quickly. 'Is it still red for you, Tom?'

Her heart skipped a beat. Unexpectedly, she wanted him to stay. She wanted time with him away from the hospital again, like they'd had on that walk through the park.

Maybe it wasn't the best idea but she wanted... what? To see a glimpse of the real Thomas again? The one that had called her 'Becca' and given her a hug?

'Sounds good,' he said. 'But I'll buy them. Can I get you something else, Matt? Alistair?'

'No, thanks,' Alistair said. 'I'll finish this but then I'd better head off, too. Got an early ward round tomorrow.'

They clinked glasses when the drinks had been poured.

'Here's to Paddington's staying exactly where it should be. For ever.'

'Paddington's,' Rebecca echoed. 'It's been quite

a fight, hasn't it? Let's hope there's no final glitch that stops it becoming official.'

'How could there be?' Matt said. 'It feels like we've got the whole of London on our side now.'

'How amazing was it for Sheikh Idris to have made that donation?' Alistair said. 'We wouldn't be celebrating now if it wasn't for him. Can you imagine being *that* rich?'

'No.' Rebecca sipped her wine. 'But I can imagine loving my daughter enough to want to thank the people who helped her. And save the place where the miracle had happened.'

Oh, help! That was a heavy thing to say, given the company. No wonder Thomas was draining his glass of wine. The bartender noticed instantly and raised a bottle as well as his eyebrows. Thomas nodded and his glass was refilled. He glanced at Rebecca's glass and then caught her gaze and she nodded acceptance of the unspoken offer.

Why not? It had been a long day and they both had things to celebrate other than a successful campaign to save the hospital they both worked in. They shared a patient who'd come through some pretty amazing surgery today.

And they were making a fresh start on their new relationship.

It was already feeling easier and Alistair had obviously noticed a difference. She hadn't missed that glance he'd shared with Matt when they'd seen them come in together and he'd made a point of telling Thomas that it was good to see him being social.

It was Rebecca that he seemed to want to talk to now, however.

'I was looking for you earlier today. Sounded like you were tied up in Theatre for a long session. Interesting case?'

'It was. You don't often get to insert a ventricular assist device.'

'Ah, that's little Penelope Craig, isn't it? I heard about that. Did it go well?'

'It's working perfectly,' Thomas put in. 'We'll just have to hope that it buys enough time for her to get a transplant.' He turned away to respond to something Matt said and, within moments, the two of them were engrossed in conversation.

Alistair was looking thoughtful as he took a step closer to Rebecca. 'That's what I was wanting to give you a heads-up about.' He lowered his voice, even though nobody would have been able to overhear their conversation in this noisy bar. 'I've got a case in ICU at the moment. Six-year-old boy. We're going to repeat tests in the next day or two but I don't think we're going to find any signs of brain activity. He could become a possible donor in the near future.'

Rebecca's nod was solemn. 'I know the case,' she said quietly.

Who didn't? This little boy—Ryan Walker— had been the most seriously injured child in the dreadful school fire at Westbourne Grove that had been the catalyst to turn the attention of the media onto the plight of Paddington Children's Hospital's impending closure. Any real recovery from his severe head injury had always been unlikely and, only a few weeks ago, he'd had a major setback with a new bleed in his brain.

He'd been on life support in the intensive care unit ever since.

If he was declared brain-dead, and his parents were willing to consider the idea of organ donation, then he would become one of Rebecca's patients. It was not often that she became involved at this stage. Retrieval of organs was usually somewhere else, from a patient whose family had already accepted that there was no hope for their own child and who had the generosity of heart to realise that their tragedy could provide hope for others.

'Have the parents been spoken to?'

'Not yet. They're still coming to terms with how bad things are. I think they're still hoping for some kind of miracle. I suspect that discussion is going to come after the next electroencephalogram. I was hoping to maybe include you in that family conference. To introduce the subject of possible organ donation?' Alistair sighed and then finished his drink. 'And now I really must get home and make sure that Claire's been putting her feet up.'

Matt followed Alistair's lead and Thomas and Rebecca found themselves alone at the bar when they'd really only started on their refilled glasses.

A waiter walked past, carrying plates from the kitchen and the smell of the hot food made Rebecca turn her head.

'Have you eaten?' Thomas asked.

'No. I didn't find the time. I'll grab a sandwich when I get home.'

'I've just realised I missed dinner, too. Not a good idea, drinking on an empty stomach.'

'No...' She'd wanted him to stay here and give them some time together, but dinner seemed like an intimate thing to do.

But friends could have dinner together, couldn't they?

Of course they could. It was what friends did.

'I think I saw some Yorkshire puddings with that roast beef that went past.'

'Oh.' Rebecca pushed any lingering doubts aside. 'I'll bet they have fish and chips with mushy peas on the menu, too.'

'Let's find out.'

Within a matter of minutes, they found themselves at a quiet corner table, menus in hand and,
a commendably short time after that, they had
delicious, hot meals in front of them.

And it was much easier than Rebecca had expected. They'd done this a million times together
in the past and they could eat and chat without
it being a big deal. They talked about Penny and
the surgery.

'I'm glad you came to watch,' she admitted.

'So am I,' Thomas said quietly. 'You've come a
long way, Becca. Did it occur to you that the last
time I watched you operate was also on Penny?
When she was about six months old?'

'Mmm...'

He hadn't been around for the last surgery on
Penny, though, had he? He'd gone by then and
had taken any hope of salvaging anything from
the wreck their marriage had become.

A silence fell between them, which made the
background conversation of other customers and
the music from the juke box increasingly notice-

able. Rebecca took a sip of her wine. And then another.

When the Ricky Martin song with its strong Latino beat started playing, the silence between them suddenly became charged.

Some memories only needed something like a few bars of a song to make it feel like they'd happened yesterday.

Salsa dance classes had been a form of exercise Thomas had been dragged along to when they were at medical school.

'It'll keep you fit,' Rebecca had assured him. *'And it's the best stress relief. Just what we'll need when it comes to exam time.'*

Who knew what an excellent dancer Thomas would turn out to be? Or how much they both found they loved it?

Rebecca hadn't danced in more than five years.

From the look on Thomas's face, neither had he.

The wine had to be blamed for the lack of thought on Rebecca's part. For the crazy urge that she couldn't suppress. Maybe it was the memory of the kind of stress relief it could provide. A cure for the slightly awkward silence? A distraction from both memories she didn't want to sink into and the prospect of the kind of conversation she might have to have with Ryan Walker's family in the near future?

'I love this song,' she heard herself say as her smile grew. 'Are you up for it?'

Friends could dance together, couldn't they? Without it being a big deal? It wasn't that much of a step up from having dinner together and that had been fine until a few moments ago. Maybe she wanted to recapture that feeling of being comfortable in each other's company.

Thomas was looking stunned. It was clearly the last thing he had expected and just as obviously he had no idea how to react.

Rebecca helped him out. She put her glass of wine down and stood up, holding out her hand, already turning towards the tiny square of a dance floor that the pub offered.

It didn't matter if he was only being polite,

so that she wouldn't be embarrassed by being the only person on the dance floor, but something inside Rebecca's chest melted as he hesitated for only a moment before following her. He touched her fingers, caught her hand in his and then pulled her close.

They could have been back in one of those Tuesday night dance classes. Or even at the one competition they'd entered, just for fun. The muscle memory came back within moments and they moved together as well as they always had. Thomas's lead was so smooth and so easy to follow that Rebecca could simply let the music flow over them and enjoy every step and twirl and dip.

It was over too soon. The next song was a slow one and the kind of dancing that would require was definitely not appropriate between friends. Rebecca didn't even risk a direct glance at Thomas as she headed back to their table.

'Thanks,' she said. 'Can't remember when I last had a dance.'

'Me, neither.'

* * *

Another silence fell. Were they both thinking back to when that might have been?

Thomas certainly was.

And it wasn't that difficult because he hadn't been anywhere near a dance floor in the last five years. Rebecca had been the last person he'd danced with.

The realisation released a flood of memories. Just snatches. How reluctant he'd been when Rebecca had come into class that day at med school, waving a flyer advertising the start of a new term for salsa classes.

The laughter and fun of those Tuesday nights when they'd both been complete beginners, fumbling their way through the steps and trying not to trip each other up.

The satisfaction of moves becoming automatic enough to be able to enjoy the music and hold Rebecca in his arms at the same time. To see the joy on her face and feel it in the response of her body.

Their wedding dance…

How much harder it had been to dance with her as her belly expanded in pregnancy but it hadn't stopped them.

There had always been music on when they were at home together. How often had they paused for a moment as they passed each other? When a brief touch or hug could morph into a dance move or two?

Gwen had loved it. As a baby she'd beam at them from her bouncy chair. As a toddler, she'd demanded to join in.

Maybe that was actually the last occasion that Thomas had danced. When he'd held the small hand of his daughter in the air so she could twirl around. When he'd scooped her into his arms and then bent down to dip her head close enough to the floor to make her shriek with laughter.

Oh, God!

That memory hurt.

Was the pain the reason his gaze sought Rebecca's? Did he need the comfort of a connection with the only other person on earth who would understand how much it hurt?

He saw the moment that connection fused. The way her eyes filled with tears.

'Oh, *Tom...*'

Her lips were trembling. He saw the first tear escape and roll down the side of her nose.

How embarrassing would it be for her to break down in front of all these people in the pub? It would be worse than finding herself alone on the dance floor. Pulling out his wallet he put down more than enough cash to cover their dinner.

'Come with me,' he said, taking her hand. 'Time we got some fresh air, I think.'

She held it together until they were out on the street. Until they'd walked far enough to be away from the sound of the regulars at the Frog and Peach enjoying their Friday night out. And then she stopped and pulled her hand from his, so that she could cover her eyes.

'I... I'm sorry,' she choked. 'It's just that I... I remembered the last time I saw you dancing...'

Thomas clenched his jaw. 'Me, too. With...with Gwen...'

The sob sounded like it was being torn from Rebecca's heart.

'Sometimes,' she whispered, 'I miss her *so* much…'

There was nothing Thomas could do other than take her in his arms. He needed to hold her. He needed someone to hold him back because those tears were contagious.

'Same,' he muttered.

They stood there for what seemed like the longest time. Against a wrought-iron fence, out of the way of people who passed with barely a glance at the embracing couple. Cars and buses and taxis thundered by on the busy road. The world continued to spin but, for Thomas, it had paused. There was nothing but this holding. And being held.

And then Rebecca shifted in his arms and looked up at him and her wet cheeks gleamed under the light of a nearby lamppost. Her eyes were huge and dark and…and so very, very sad.

There was nothing Thomas could do other than to dip his head and kiss her.

Gently.

Slowly.

With enough tenderness to let her know that he understood.

That he felt exactly the same way.

CHAPTER SEVEN

THIS WAS WHAT had been missing from her life for so long.

Being held when she felt so sad.

Knowing that someone else understood how she felt.

Rebecca closed her eyes and fell into that kiss. There was no way she was going to question the wisdom of what was happening or what the consequences might be.

She'd been waiting for this moment for ever. She just hadn't realised it.

That touch of lips on hers was so heartbreakingly tender it should have made her want to cry but, instead, it covered the source of the tears that had already been falling and smothered them like sand on the embers of a fire.

It was the feeling that someone genuinely cared about her.

Loved her, even…

No. Not *someone*. There was only one person who had ever made her feel quite like this. Only one person who could really understand exactly how she felt, because he had been there and he felt the same way.

Tom…

The name escaped her lips on a sigh but Rebecca didn't realise it was audible until she felt the change in the way she was being held. The tension in the muscles of his arms was instant—preparation for being taken away?

Yes. Thomas was letting her go as she opened her eyes. He was turning his head, too, but not before she'd seen the glint of tears in his eyes and something that looked a lot like…regret?

And then he ran his fingers through his hair, raising his face to the streetlamp above them. His eyes were tightly shut.

'Sorry,' he muttered. 'I shouldn't have done that.'

Why not?

Because it meant that he was throwing away the rule book about keeping so much distance between them?

Because he had another partner that he'd just cheated on? The lines of pain on his face suggested that that was the more likely explanation.

The chill that ran down Rebecca's spine actually made her shiver. But she was still aware of the warmth that kiss had delivered. The comfort of feeling that he still cared.

Did *she* still care? Judging by the urge to erase those lines of pain around his eyes and mouth, apparently she did.

'It's okay, Tom.' Rebecca touched his arm. 'We were both upset. It's my fault. I... I shouldn't have asked you to dance. Dragged us both back into the past like that.'

He opened his eyes and looked down at her and she could see nothing but sadness in his eyes.

'It never goes away, does it?'

'No.' But Rebecca pulled in a deeper breath. 'It

does change, though. It gets less painful. There are good things to remember, too.'

His nod was slow. One corner of his mouth lifted a little.

'Yeah…like how much she loved to dance. She was such a happy little thing, wasn't she?'

Rebecca nodded. Gwen had been the happiest of children. She would wake up with a smile on her face and her arms outstretched to greet the people she loved and the new day that would always bring excitement. And she spread that happiness around her with such abundance that anybody nearby would catch it and then give it back and it would get bigger every time.

The world without Gwen had lost so much light. It was still dark in places and Rebecca knew it wouldn't help to step any closer to those corners. It wouldn't help her and it might well drive Thomas back to where he'd been—unable to find any way out.

'It's okay,' she said again. 'It didn't mean anything more than sharing a memory. It…it wasn't cheating or anything.'

'*Cheating?*' Had Thomas taken a step back or did it just feel like he had? 'What's that supposed to mean?'

Rebecca bit her lip. This was really overstepping boundaries. A shared past was something they couldn't avoid but Thomas had been very clear that his current personal life was out of bounds. They were just beginning to feel their way into what could become a friendship. Making a reference to his sex life was more than awkward.

It was excruciating.

He was still waiting for a response. Frowning, now, as if he was fitting pieces of a difficult puzzle together.

'Did you feel like *you* were cheating?' he asked quietly. 'Are you...*with* someone, Becca?'

'*No!*' The word came out more vehemently than she had intended. As if the idea of being with someone was shocking. She followed it with a huff that sounded incredulous. 'Not me, I thought *you* might be...'

There was a long moment of silence. Rebecca

shivered again and wrapped her arms around her body. She didn't dare meet his gaze. Instead, she turned her head to look along the footpath. In the direction she needed to take to go home.

To escape?

Thomas cleared his throat. 'I'm not,' he said. 'Are you?'

Rebecca raised her gaze. 'No.'

Their gazes held. The question they both wanted to ask hung like a cartoon bubble over their heads. Until they both spoke at the same time.

'Has there been…?'

'Have you…?'

Another pause. And then it happened again.

'No,' they said in unison.

The silence had a stunned echo to it this time. It was Rebecca who broke it.

'Why not?' she whispered.

'Why?' he countered.

'Because…because it's been five years. And I know… I know how lonely it can get.'

Thomas looked away. 'Guess I haven't been

ready,' he said. 'I focused on work enough for that to be all that mattered.'

'Me, too,' Rebecca admitted. 'And the time just kept going past. I'd forgotten how long it was until…until you came back to Paddington's. I guess I've just taken things day by day for so long, it's become engrained. I never look too far into the future.'

'And I discovered that it's better never to look too far into the past.'

Rebecca felt herself become very still. This was a huge admission, wasn't it?

She hadn't felt this close to Thomas since… well, maybe since the very early days of their relationship. When it had been so easy to say anything and trust that it would be accepted and understood. When anything seemed possible and glowed with the prospect of real happiness.

It had been a very different kind of closeness at the end—during those awful days when they'd sat in the intensive care unit beside Gwen's bed. Holding each other's hands so tightly that it could become painful—but never as painful as what was happening around them. That connection had been more powerful, perhaps, but far less happy.

With the embrace of that dance still lingering on her skin, Rebecca chose to tap into that first memory of the connection they'd discovered with each other. It made it feel so natural to say more.

'We're both stuck, aren't we?' she suggested softly. 'Living in the present.'

'It's not a bad place to be.'

'But we're still young. There's a lot more to life than work…'

Thomas moved his head in another one of those slow, thoughtful nods. He even offered her the ghost of another smile.

'Like dancing?'

Rebecca smiled back and mirrored his nod.

'I'll keep that in mind.' His faint smile vanished. 'It's getting late. I'll walk you home.'

'No need. It's out of your way. I can get a cab.'

'At this time on a Friday night? You'll be lucky.'

Rebecca wanted to agree. She wanted to walk with Thomas and keep talking. If they did, maybe she could find that connection that seemed to have vanished again.

Or had she imagined it?

Fate intervened in any case. A black cab was heading towards them, with its yellow light glowing to advertise its availability. Thomas raised his arm and it pulled into the curb.

'There you go. I was wrong…' His smile was tight. Relieved? He wanted to get away, didn't he? So that he didn't have to revisit any more painful memories? Or to admit he might have been wrong about anything else—like the way he'd abandoned her when she'd needed him more than ever?

Rebecca opened the back door of the cab. 'Want to share?'

She could feel his hesitation. She saw him open his mouth as if he was about to accept the invitation. And then his expression changed—as though he'd just walked into a mental brick wall.

One of those well-built barriers?

'I'll walk.' His voice had a gruff edge. 'I need the exercise after those Yorkshire puddings.'

She turned her head as the cab pulled away. She could see Thomas through the back window, already heading in the opposite direction.

Alone.

Going back to his apartment where he would still be alone.

As she would when she got back to hers.

It felt wrong.

A lot more wrong than it would have felt last week. Or even yesterday.

She hadn't been wrong about finding that connection again, had she? It was bigger than simply the fact that they'd kissed each other. Or admitted that there'd been no one else in their lives since their marriage ended.

Something had shifted in the layers that had been used to bury what had been their marriage. Had Thomas seen the same glint of what had been uncovered?

Did he realise that the connection they'd had was still there?

That it was possible that it might actually be even stronger?

That wasn't the real question, though, was it?

Rebecca felt suddenly weary enough to rest her head on the back of the seat and close her eyes.

The real question was whether he would want to uncover any more of what had been buried for so long. Whether she wanted that herself.

'And I discovered that it's better never to look too far into the past.'

You wouldn't find anything if you chose not to look. And you could make it easy not to see by kicking the layers back into place.

She hadn't intended to force either of them to look tonight. Asking him to dance had been impulsive and the shared memories that it had provoked had been inevitable.

Had it made things harder?

Judging by the ache in her own heart, Rebecca suspected that it had.

That ache suggested that she'd never really stopped loving Thomas. Getting closer to him again could mean that she was setting herself up for a whole new heartbreak—one that could mean she would be stuck for even longer.

Alone. With no partner in her current life or dreams of a family in her future.

Something like a groan escaped along with her sigh.

'You all right, love?'

Rebecca opened her eyes to see the cab driver watching her in his rear-view mirror.

'Almost there,' he added cheerfully. 'You'll be home before you know it.'

She summoned a smile and turned her head in time to see the signpost of her street flash past.

This was where she lived.

But it wasn't a home any more. Not really.

Work was failing to provide the complete distraction that Thomas Wolfe had come to depend on.

He'd spent most of his weekend at the hospital and most of that in his office, writing an article for a paediatric cardiology journal on the relationship between the diagnosis of asthma and dilated cardiomyopathy. He took his time over ward rounds on both Saturday and Sunday mornings but his visits to the intensive care unit were very brief.

Penny was the patient in most need of frequent monitoring but, theoretically, she was under the care of her surgical team at the moment and wouldn't be transferred back to the cardiology ward until Rebecca was happy with her condition. He was on call, of course, if any consultation was needed but, so far, everything was going very smoothly. They'd kept her asleep a little longer than planned but her sedation was now being gradually lifted and it was hoped that she would be awake and ready to move to the ward first thing on Monday morning.

His visits to the unit hadn't coincided with any that Rebecca might be making and that was probably a good thing because Thomas wasn't sure he was ready to see her again just yet.

What had happened on Friday night was still doing his head in. Thoughts kept intruding, even when he should have been completely engrossed in his writing.

*A diagnosis of moderate persistent bron-
chial asthma was made in the four-year-old
girl. A year later she was admitted with fea-
tures of an acute exacerbation, including
breathlessness, cough, sleep disturbances
and poor response to nebulised salbutamol...*

His gaze drifted to the series of chest X-rays he
was planning to include in the next section, but
he wasn't looking at the evidence of fluid build-
up in the lungs.

It was that kiss that was the problem.

Or maybe it had been the dancing.

Then again, he kept remembering—with a
slight sense of shock—that Rebecca had told him
she was single. That she hadn't been with anyone
else in the last five years.

Why not?

It couldn't have been because of any lack of
interest on the part of the men she must have
encountered. She was gorgeous. Clever. Funny.
Such a positive person, too. That was where
Gwen's sunny nature had come from. Rebecca
had a smile that could light up a room and she

automatically looked for the bright side of anything, no matter how bad it was.

Even when it was the worst thing imaginable. She'd been the one to bring up the awful subject of organ donation, when they'd been sitting so helplessly, day after day, beside the bedside of their critically injured daughter.

'If there's even the shadow of something good that could come out of this,' she'd said, *'maybe it's the fact that the lives of other people's precious children could be saved.'*

She'd been the one who had arranged Gwen's funeral. The tiny pink casket with bright flowers painted all over it. The pink and white balloons that were released that contained little packets of wildflower seeds. The songs that had come from beloved television shows and Disney movies.

'It's the last party I can ever give her,' she'd said. *'I want it to be what would have made her happy.'*

Oh, God…

So many memories were coming out of the woodwork. He tried to shake them off before that lump in his throat made it too hard to breathe. Before he had to fight back tears, the way he had when he'd made the mistake of kissing Rebecca and could feel the grief of losing her—and Gwen—doing its best to wrap his heart in those vicious tentacles all over again.

But why was she still alone?

She hadn't blamed herself for the accident. She certainly hadn't blamed him. She hadn't even blamed the nursery school who had been responsible for Gwen's safety that day.

She'd moved on. She'd been able to keep working with children. More than that, she'd become involved with the whole transplant side of medicine and even changed the direction of her own career to become as involved as it was possible to get.

If she could handle the emotional side of that, why hadn't she moved on enough to find a new partner? To start a new family, even, which had always been her dream of the perfect future.

There was only one answer that Thomas could come up with.

He'd hurt her so badly, she simply didn't want to risk it again.

And yet, here she was trying to establish a friendship with him. She seemed to want to spend time with him and it had definitely been her idea to have that dance.

It didn't make sense.

She'd accused him of running away. Of leaving their marriage even while they'd still been together.

Did this mean that she was prepared to forgive him?

That it was possible there was more than friendship to be salvaged from the wreck of their lives together?

It had felt like that, when he'd been holding her in his arms while she cried.

When he'd kissed her and felt her kissing him back.

But it was doing his head in.

Part of him wanted nothing more than a second chance.

Part of him wanted to keep well clear of all those memories to protect himself.

But another part still cared enough to be determined not to hurt Rebecca again. He'd failed her once before and it certainly hadn't been intentional. How could he be sure that it wouldn't happen again?

It would be better for everybody if he dismissed the possibility.

He carried on writing.

Respiratory distress worsened to the point that mechanical ventilation was required. The most likely diagnosis considered at this stage included complicated severe asthma, infection, fluid overload and underlying cardiac disease...

His hands stilled again as he lost the thread of his next sentence. Shutting his eyes for a moment, Thomas tried to force himself to focus. This article was taking a lot longer than usual to pull together but he would get it done; he just needed more time.

And that was the answer to a lot of things, wasn't it?

More time.

He could step back from the confusion that a friendship with his ex-wife was causing. Given time, he would be able to think more clearly and decide what the best course of action might be. It seemed that trying to set her free by ending their marriage hadn't worked but something needed to happen so that they could both move on in their personal lives.

By finding new partners?

Thomas could feel himself scowling at a computer screen covered with words that were no more than a blur.

He didn't want a new partner.

Worse than that, the thought of Rebecca with someone else was…unacceptable?

Oh, man, his head really was a mess. And it was starting to interfere with his work.

How had he managed to keep his personal head space successfully separated from anything professional for the last five years?

Because he had been a long way away from Rebecca, that was why. He hadn't had to see her every day. To talk to her and watch her work. He hadn't spent any time with her alone.

And he hadn't even *thought* about dancing with her, let alone kissing her.

Okay, so that wasn't completely true.

With a sigh, Thomas saved his file and closed the programme. He needed some fresh air. A brisk walk or maybe a run that would not only distract him, it might tire him out enough to sleep properly tonight.

A long run. All the way around Regent's Park and Primrose Hill, perhaps.

No. Too many memories, including some very recent ones.

Hyde Park, then. It was closer, bigger and far less familiar.

Safer. For both himself and the woman he had loved so totally.

It was exactly what he had always vowed to do. To put Rebecca's needs above his own.

To keep her safe.

* * *

Any working week in a field of medicine that included critically unwell patients was a roller-coaster of good moments, worrying moments and—at the bottom of one of those loops—the really heartbreaking moments that made you wonder if you were up to the kind of stress this job could entail.

Rebecca was about to face one of those low swoops and she had to gather every ounce of her courage to do it.

Walking away from one of the good moments was making it harder. She had just come from the paediatric cardiology ward where her visit to Penelope Craig had coincided with Thomas doing his ward round.

The smile with which he had greeted her had been a relief. She'd barely seen him all week and had convinced herself that she'd wrecked any chance of friendship between them after that night at the Frog and Peach.

Dancing with him, for heaven's sake.

Crying on his shoulder. Was it really so surprising that he'd tried to comfort her by kissing her? It hadn't meant anything but it could well have been enough to have him raise those barriers between them again.

But he'd smiled at her as she entered Penny's room and it hadn't just been a polite greeting. There was a warmth in his eyes that said he was happy to see her. Had he noticed that their paths hadn't crossed in so many days?

Perhaps he thought she'd been deliberately avoiding him and he was relieved, as well. The truth was that Rebecca had been flat out. The Teddy Bears' Picnic was happening this coming weekend and the last minute organisation had taken up every spare second she'd had, and then some, including several very late nights.

So she was weary, and that always accentuated any emotional components of her job.

Everybody was smiling in Penny's room this morning.

'So she can come home next week?' Julia asked. 'And she doesn't need to be on oxygen all the time?'

'Not unless she's getting breathless or becomes unwell,' Thomas told her. 'And that's looking less likely every day.'

'And we can let her do whatever she wants? Go back to school?'

'Not just yet. We'll keep her in until after the weekend and see how she's doing and then we'll talk about school. Let her walk around as much as she wants to and you could take her to the playground.'

'I can dance,' Penny told Rebecca. 'Just like Sapphire Ballerina Bear. Want to see?' She scrambled off her mother's lap, put her arms in the air and turned herself in a slightly wobbly circle. She didn't seem to be in any significant pain as she bounced back from her major surgery. The grin on her face made everybody smile all over again.

'That's fantastic,' Rebecca said. She held out the object in her hand to Julia. 'This is for you. Keep it with you at all times from now on.'

'Oh…' Julia's gaze sought that of her husband and her glance was fearful.

'It's the pager,' Peter said.

'Yes. Penny's on the top of the transplant list now and a new heart could become available at any time. If it does, even if it's somewhere else in the country, you'll get paged and you'll need to come back to the hospital immediately. That doesn't mean that the transplant will definitely go ahead because sometimes unexpected things happen but you'll need to be here and be prepared. We repeat a lot of tests to make sure nothing's changed.'

Julia and Peter both nodded solemnly.

'In the meantime...' Rebecca smiled at Penny who was twirling again. 'Enjoy everything that you haven't been able to do for so long. I'll come back again before you go home in case you have any questions but you've got my phone number, too. Don't hesitate to call.'

'Thank you so much, Dr Scott,' Peter said. 'You have no idea how much this means to us all.'

'Oh, I think I do.' The glance in Thomas's direction happened without thinking and the look in his eyes was better than any smile. They both knew how precious for Julia and Peter this time with their daughter would be. They both knew they were providing a gift they'd never been able to receive themselves.

The connection was most definitely still there.

And, regardless of whether either of them would choose for it to happen or not, it seemed to be getting stronger.

So it was no wonder that her next appointment was a prospect that weighed down both her feet and her heart. She could feel both getting heavier as she slid away from the joy of Penny's visit to the sadness that she knew she would find in the quiet space of the most private room of the paediatric intensive care unit, where six-year-old Ryan Walker had been declared brain-dead late yesterday afternoon.

Alistair North was waiting for her outside the unit.

'Ryan's parents are with him at the moment. They were present for the second round of tests last night and they've been here ever since. I paged you when they were ready to ask about what's going to happen next.'

Rebecca nodded. As a doctor who worked in the field of organ transplants, she was not allowed to have anything to do with the range of tests conducted to confirm brain death. These were normally done twice, by two different doctors, spaced apart by at least twelve hours.

'No inconclusive results, then?'

Alistair shook his head, his face sombre. 'I think it was the angiography that hit them the hardest. The image is so clear when all you've got is a dark space inside the skull with absolutely no blood flow.'

Rebecca nodded. She knew exactly how devastating that kind of image could be.

'His grandparents are in one of the relatives' rooms, looking after his little sister, Gemma.'

Alistair introduced her to Louise and Colin Walker, Ryan's parents, who were sitting, their hands linked and their faces pale with shock, beside his bed.

Wisps of red hair showed under the bandages

on Ryan's head and his freckles stood out on a pale little face. Only six years old, this was a tragedy that touched everybody's hearts.

'I'm so very, very sorry,' she said quietly. 'I haven't been involved with Ryan's care since his accident but I know that everything possible was done.'

They both nodded but Colin was frowning. He didn't understand why she was here.

'You asked about what happens next,' Alistair said. 'So there are decisions that need to be made. Difficult decisions.' He cleared his throat. 'I asked Dr Scott—Rebecca—to come because she's had a lot of experience with supporting people to make these kinds of decisions.'

'You mean about…about when we turn off the life support?' Louise's voice broke and she covered her eyes with her hands. 'And what…what happens then?'

'There's no hurry,' Rebecca said gently. 'We can give you all the time you need. And all the support you—and the rest of your family—might find helpful.'

'Rebecca is a surgeon,' Alistair continued quietly. 'There's never a good time to introduce a subject like this, but she's the head of our transplant team. She's come to talk to you about the possibility of Ryan being an organ donor.'

Colin Walker's face became even paler as he joined the dots. 'No,' he whispered. 'How could you even ask?'

'I understand,' Rebecca said into the horrified silence. 'I'm not here to do anything more than introduce myself at the moment. To leave you with some information and my phone number. You can call me anytime at all—day or night— if you have any questions or need to talk.'

Colin couldn't look at her and Louise still had her hands over her face.

'All I ask is that you think about it,' she added softly. 'And I can tell you that the gift of life *can* help—for both sides.'

She glanced at Alistair and he nodded. It was time for her to leave and not seem to be putting any pressure at all on these grieving parents. The subject had been raised and Alistair and the team in the intensive care unit would continue to care for Ryan until they were ready to make their decision.

Walking through the double doors to leave the unit, Rebecca could see a woman coming out of one of the relatives' rooms, holding the hand of a small girl who had bright red curly hair and a freckled button nose. About two years old, she had to be Gemma—Ryan Walker's little sister. Rebecca smiled at the grandmother but kept going. This wasn't the time to introduce herself to the wider family.

It was good that Ryan wasn't an only child. Not that that could change how devastating this whole situation was but Rebecca had thought more than once over the years she'd been involved in this specialty that it could make a real difference in the future. She'd seen it happen on the rare occasions when she'd become involved at this earlier stage of the process of organ donation. These parents were forced to carry on. To stay engaged with all aspects of life—including each other?

Every time, it made her wonder whether that

would have made a difference to herself and Thomas and she would feel a beat of her own loss. Not just for Gwen, or for their marriage, but for the larger family that could have been.

She paused in front of the elevators, closing her eyes against the pain of it all.

Maybe Thomas hadn't been so wrong, after all, to distance himself from having to experience it again and again.

She wanted to tell him that. To tell him that she understood. More than she had at the time.

That she could forgive him…

No. Right now she didn't want to talk to him.

She just wanted him to hold her in his arms and comfort her. To remind her that they'd done the right thing when they hadn't hesitated to agree to donate Gwen's organs. When they'd known that they wouldn't be able to hold their precious daughter when she took her last breath.

They would only be able to hold each other.

CHAPTER EIGHT

'I UNDERSTAND.' REBECCA gave Louise Walker's hand a squeeze. 'It's okay.'

Louise looked up at the clock on the wall of this private room. 'Colin will be back soon. He's collecting his parents from the airport. They were on a cruise ship so we've had to wait until they got to a port.'

'He doesn't know that you asked to meet me?'

The distressed young mother shook her head. 'He doesn't want to talk about any of it. Turning off the life support is bad enough but the idea of organ donation is too much for him.'

'I do understand.'

'But I want to do it,' Louise whispered, tears streaming down her face. 'I keep thinking, what if Ryan was the one who was really sick and needed a new heart or lungs or something? If I was one of those parents who was hoping, every day, that a miracle would happen and that an organ would become available…'

'There are two sides to every story,' Rebecca agreed quietly. 'But everybody feels differently and it would be very wrong to try and force Colin to agree to something he can't handle.'

'Dr North says we can take a few days but… it's so hard. Part of me just wants it to be over, you know? So that we can start trying to put our lives back together.'

'I understand,' Rebecca said again. 'And I don't want you to feel guilty about not making a decision. Or making the decision for Ryan not to be a donor. It's something the whole family needs to be sure about.'

'I know my parents think it's a good thing— that something good could still come out of this whole horrible accident. All these weeks we've had hoping for the impossible.'

Rebecca had to blink away the sudden moisture in her own eyes. Along with the echo of her own broken voice from so long ago.

'If there's even the shadow of something good that could come out of this, maybe it's the fact that the lives of other people's precious children could be saved.'

'I think Colin's parents might, too,' Louise added. 'We're all going to come in and spend time with Ryan over the weekend. That will be the time to talk about it again.'

'You've got my number. If I can support you in any way—with whatever decision you make—please call me.'

'I will. And thank you.' She looked up at the clock again. 'I'd better get back. Mum wants to get home so they can take Gemma to the zoo this afternoon. Weird, isn't it? But life doesn't stop, even when it feels like the world should have stopped turning for a while.'

Rebecca let go of her hand, noting how pale and exhausted Louise was looking. 'Have you been away from here at all yourself?'

Louise shook her head. 'Every minute counts, doesn't it?'

The two women parted at the door. Impulsively, Louise hugged Rebecca.

'I think you do really understand,' she whispered. 'It means a lot.'

Rebecca hugged her back. This part of her job often entailed an emotional connection to patients and their families that went above and beyond normal boundaries. Not that she'd ever tell people that she'd been through the same thing herself because that could be a form of pressure to follow her example. That her understanding was genuine seemed to come through unspoken, however, and it was reassuring both to the families she worked with and to herself.

She brought something to this job that nobody else could. It was what she was meant to be doing and she was proud of the difference she could make in the lives of others.

That pride was normally a very private thing that came in moments like this. A public acknowledgement like the one that was to be celebrated at the Teddy Bears' Picnic was very different. Accolades were unnecessary—embarrassing, even—

but any discomfort was outweighed by the joy of being with so many people who'd had their lives transformed by organ donation. There was a real need for public education, too, and this year was even more important given the spotlight that Paddington's was still under.

As the head of the transplant team, Rebecca knew that she would be under her own spotlight and she knew the responsibility that she carried. Transplant surgery entailed the kind of drama that people loved to hear about. Showcasing Paddington as an important centre with a track record of great success could confirm how necessary it was for this hospital to remain for generations to come. It could be the final push that would mean its safety was officially guaranteed.

It was a perfect day for the big event.

Not that Thomas had intended to go, but everybody had been talking about it when he'd been in at work doing his usual ward round.

'They want as many Paddington's staff members there as possible, to show how united we all are,' Rosie had told him as she accompanied him to Penny's room. Julia was apparently worried that her daughter was coming down with a cold or something that might delay the possibility of her going home.

'I'm going to meet Leo there, as soon as my shift finishes,' Rosie continued. 'The twins have got their teddies ready for the "best dressed" bear competition at the end of the day and they're so excited by the prospect of a pony ride. It'll be such fun!'

'The Teddy Bears' picnic?' Julia Craig overheard the end of the conversation at they entered her room. 'I wish we could go. Next year.' She smiled at Penny. 'You could take Sapphire.'

'I want to go now,' Penny said. 'I want a pony ride, too.'

'Let's see how you are,' Thomas said. 'Mummy says you've got a sniffle.'

It wasn't anything to worry about but the Craig family wouldn't be attending the picnic this time. Maybe it was knowing that Rebecca would be there that tipped the balance as Thomas left Paddington's early in the afternoon.

It had been so good to see her yesterday when she'd given Penny's parents that significant pager. To see her return his smile and feel like it was still possible that they could be friends without his head getting so messed up.

That they could rewind a little? To forget that dance. And the kiss.

To start again with some better boundaries in place?

Besides, the day was too perfect to spend either in his office finishing that article or stuck in that shoebox of an apartment that had no view of anything green. Thomas pulled off his tie and opened the top button of his shirt. He rolled his sleeves up and kept walking, taking the same route that he and Rebecca had taken that first time they'd spent some real time together since his return.

The sun shone from a cloudless sky but the slopes of Primrose Hill caught a breeze that kept the temperature pleasant enough for the children to enjoy even the more strenuous activities available, like the egg and spoon races and the obstacle course. Thomas walked past the team of volunteers cooking sausages on barbecues and the gazebo that had a queue of children waiting their turn for face painting. He could see a trio of fat, little ponies that had another queue of excited children waiting and he could hear gleeful shrieks coming from inside the bouncy castle.

There were cameras and reporters everywhere, from television stations, both local and national newspapers and magazines.

And there was Rebecca, looking absolutely gorgeous in blue jeans and a white, short-sleeved shirt that had a teddy bear print on it. She had her long, dark hair tied back but it wasn't wrapped up into a knot like it would be at work. It hung down her back in a wavy ponytail that was being teased in the breeze.

She hadn't seen him, because she was focused on the woman she was talking to, and he was partly screened by the man with a huge camera balanced on his shoulder and a young lad who was holding a fluffy microphone on a stick close to the two women. Thomas was simply one of the group of interested onlookers who were watching this interview. He edged a little closer so that he could hear what Rebecca was saying.

'So three people in the UK die every day because of this shortage. At the moment there are over six thousand people on the transplant waiting list and about two hundred of them are children. And many of those children come to Paddington Children's Hospital because we're one of only a few major centres for paediatric transplantation.'

'But there are organs that could be available, aren't there?' the interviewer asked. 'Is it that people don't know it's possible to donate them? Or do they not *want* to?'

'It's complicated,' Rebecca said, 'and it's a difficult subject to even think about for people who are facing the heartbreak of losing a loved one.'

'What is it that you—and all the other doctors

and medical staff here from Paddington's—want to happen? We've got a lot of people watching what's happening here. What would you tell them was the purpose of a day like today?'

'Today is about celebrating life.' Rebecca's smile lit up her face. 'Of letting the families that take that amazingly generous step of making organ donation possible realise just how much of a difference they can make to so many lives.' Her gaze shifted as she waved her arm towards the huge crowd of people around them and then it caught as she spotted Thomas.

She didn't break her speech. 'We want people to talk about it. We all think that the sort of terrible situations that lead to organ donation won't happen to us—that they only happen to other people.'

Her gaze was holding Thomas's.

'But, sadly, they do happen to some of us. And if we talk about it before they happen, it might help us make a decision that can change the world for others.'

'I'm Angela Marton and we've been talking

to Dr Rebecca Scott.' The interviewer turned to face the camera. 'That's an important message for all of us. And now let's go and meet some of the children and their families here today whose worlds *have* been changed.'

She led her crew away and the onlookers drifted in other directions but Thomas stayed where he was. He was still holding Rebecca's gaze and neither of them were smiling. The moment was, in fact, very close to being tear-jerking.

He began stepping closer at precisely the same moment Rebecca did.

His voice, when he managed to find some words, was raw.

'We did do the right thing, didn't we?'

She knew that he was talking about Gwen. About the decision they'd made to donate *her* organs.

'Absolutely,' she whispered. 'I'm proud of it… aren't you?'

Thomas had to swallow the huge lump in his throat. 'I think I am,' he said softly. 'I've never thought of it like that before.'

Rebecca's smile was as soft as her gaze. In that moment, that look felt as tender and loving as he remembered it being when they were first in love.

'I'm so glad you came today,' she said.

Thomas cleared his throat. 'Me, too.'

He wanted to sink into that soft gaze. To pull it around him for comfort like the softest blanket on the coldest night.

'Want an ice cream? Or a sausage? They're really good.'

Her smile widened until it was as bright as the one she'd given the television crew when she'd said that today was about celebrating life. Their poignant moment of connection was still there, but—as always—Rebecca was finding something positive to move towards.

And he was happy to follow her lead.

'Actually, I'm starving. A sausage sounds perfect.'

How amazing was it that Thomas had come this afternoon?

This was huge.

A lot bigger than Thomas himself probably realised, despite his admission that he had gained a new perspective, but Rebecca wasn't going to allow the beat of fear to diminish the joy that this gathering always bestowed. Having Thomas by her side only made it all the more important to focus on the positive.

It wasn't difficult. Everywhere they went, people came to greet them, eager to share news.

'Dr Scott, remember Tyler?'

The sturdy boy wearing the colours of his favourite football team ducked his head, hiding beneath the brim of his baseball cap. An older brother slung a protective arm over his shoulders.

'Tyler! Of course I remember you. Didn't you move to Manchester?' Rebecca laughed. 'Silly me. I should have recognised the jersey.' She looked up at the boy's parents. 'It's been, what... three years since Tyler's transplant? How's he doing?'

'He made it onto the junior football team last season,' his dad said proudly. 'Got player of the week twice.'

'Wow.' Rebecca looked suitably impressed. 'And you've come all the way to London just for today?'

'We had a minibus,' Tyler's mother told her. 'We belong to a support group for transplant families and we all decided to come for a day out. Tyler and his brother here have been practising to enter the three-legged race. We didn't realise how big it would be, though. Isn't it amazing how many kids there are that probably wouldn't even be alive if they hadn't had transplants?'

'It certainly is.' Thomas joined the conversation. 'But I bet there aren't too many who are player of the week in a football team.'

She introduced Thomas to Tyler's family. A few minutes later, she introduced him to Madeline's family and they learned how her life had changed since her lung transplant two years ago. Stephen was another cystic fibrosis patient who'd received his heart and lung transplant only last year. Piper had been given a kidney as a live donation from her father.

And then there was Ava.

'Rebecca.' Ava's mother, Jude, enveloped her in a hug. 'It's been way too long.'

'I know, I'm sorry. I've been meaning to call you but life's been a bit crazy what with all the organisation for today on top of everything else.' Rebecca's heart skipped a beat as she turned to include Thomas. Would Jude guess? More alarmingly, would Thomas guess that this was anything more than a doctor/patient relationship?

'This is Thomas Wolfe,' she said, the light tone of her voice sounding a bit forced to her own ears. 'He's a cardiothoracic surgeon at Paddington's. He left London before you moved here so he doesn't know Ava yet.'

He doesn't know anything about Ava, she added silently. And he doesn't need to. Not now.

Possibly not ever...

'I think we've got an outpatient appointment coming up with you, soon.' Jude held out her hand. 'Pleased to meet you, Thomas.'

'Likewise. And you, Ava.' Thomas was smiling at the tall twelve-year-old who had long blonde braids and astonishingly blue eyes. 'That's a very well-dressed bear you've got there.'

'It was my grandma's,' Ava told him shyly. 'It was Grandee's idea to give him the waistcoat and monocle. She said he needed to be old-fashioned because he's an antique. Like Grandee.'

'He's going into the competition for Best-Dressed Bear,' Ava's father added. 'Hadn't we better go and get him entered?'

'We won't hold you up.' Rebecca hoped she didn't sound as relieved as she suddenly felt. 'The speeches are going to start soon, too, and I think I need to introduce some of the speakers.'

'You *are* going to come to my birthday party, aren't you?' Ava said as the family began to move on. 'It's a special one.'

'I know, sweetheart. Thirteen. How does it feel to be almost a teenager?'

Ava shrugged. 'Okay, I guess. At least I'll be allowed to get my ears pierced. *Finally...*' She rolled her eyes at her mother.

Rebecca and Jude shared a smile. Teenage angst starting already?

'It's not far away. What can I bring?' Rebecca asked.

'Nothing but yourself. It's just family.' Jude hugged her again. 'We'll have a proper catch-up, then.'

She got a hug from Ava, as well, and then Rebecca watched them walk away for a little too long. Because she could feel Thomas staring at her? Of course he was. How many patients' families made it clear that they considered their doctor to be a member of their family?

He walked with her towards the main stage where preparations were going on for the guest speakers.

'Ava looks well,' he said, finally. 'How long ago did she get her transplant?'

Rebecca's mouth went a little dry. She tried to keep her tone casual. 'Oh, quite a few years ago now.'

'Did you do her surgery?'

'No...um...they were living in Newcastle then so the transplant was done there. Ava's dad got offered a new—and much better—job last year and it was partly because she could continue her care at Paddington's that they took it.'

'How come you know them so well?' he asked then. 'How did you meet them?'

She couldn't tell him. Did Thomas even know that it was possible for members of a donor's family to initiate contact with organ recipients through the intermediary of the transplant association? That the families could meet if both sides wanted to? Would she ever be able to tell him what an emotional journey it had been to meet the little girl who had received Gwen's heart and how they had welcomed her into their family with such love?

How healing it had been for her?

Janice, the president of the picnic committee, was rushing towards them, a clipboard in her hand that she was waving over her head.

'Yoo-hoo! Rebecca!'

But Rebecca had stopped walking. Because Thomas had stopped and one glance at his face told her that he had put two and two together. He looked as if he'd just been punched in the gut and had frozen completely to try not to collapse from the pain.

'Oh, my God…' he said. 'You know who Ava's donor was, don't you?'

Rebecca said nothing. The noises around her faded to a faint hum. She couldn't say anything.

She didn't need to.

Thomas had gone as white as a sheet.

For a long moment they simply stared at each other. She could feel his shock. The unbearable pain of knowing that a part of his daughter was in another little girl who got to dress up her teddy bear and have a family day out in the summer sunshine.

When, if life was remotely fair, it should have been Gwen.

And then he simply turned and walked away, disappearing into the crowd before Rebecca even had time to blink.

'Oh, thank goodness,' Janice said behind her. 'I've been looking for you everywhere. Are you ready to introduce the speakers? There's a radio station that wants to interview you, as well.'

Desperately, Rebecca tried to catch a glimpse of Thomas. If ever there was a time they needed to talk, this was it. A time to talk. To hold each other and cry…

And it was impossible.

She had duties she had to attend to. Being the face of transplants at Paddington's wasn't an ego trip. She was representing a hospital in desperate need of the final green light for its survival and she had the chance to say something about that before she introduced those speakers. To thank so many people who had contributed to the campaign and made this an issue that was so much bigger than a local community.

She had to do her bit to save the hospital she loved and believed in.

But what about the man that she had also loved and believed in once? The realisation that this wasn't simply that she cared about him the way she might care for any close friend made her catch her breath.

She *still* loved him…

Still believed in him…

Even a glance might be enough to convey how important that connection still was.

But Thomas was nowhere to be seen.

He had to keep moving.

If he stopped, he'd have to think and Thomas didn't want to think. He didn't want to feel the horror of that realisation all over again.

He'd known there was something odd about Rebecca's connection to that family from the moment they'd spotted each other. She was a part of that family, wasn't she?

Literally. Some of her genes were part of that pretty little girl with the long braids and big, blue eyes.

Some of *his* genes were, too.

It was too much.

She should have warned him. If he'd known, he would never have gone near that picnic today. Oh, he'd known that somewhere out there were several children who'd received the gift of Gwen's organs and he genuinely hoped they were all doing well. But to know who any of them were? To be a part of their lives and watch them growing up, when you couldn't help but think about what your own child might be doing at the age she would be now?

The pain was unbearable and all he could do was try and walk it off.

An hour passed and then another. Thomas wasn't even noticing where he walked. Around the circumference of Regent's Park. Through city streets. Right around Hyde Park. Twice.

He was thirsty. His feet and his legs ached but his heart ached more. So he kept walking until the sun was low in the sky and this day was finally drawing to a close. A day he never wanted to remember.

Exhaustion was helping because he was too tired to think coherently. Too tired to have taken any notice of where he'd been walking for the last hour but it was another shock to realise the automatic route his subconscious had dictated.

He was in his old street. Only a lamppost away from the railings and steps that led down to that basement apartment where he'd lived with Rebecca.

With Gwen…

The pain felt more like anger now.

This was Rebecca's fault. She could have warned him. Could have saved him the agony of these last few hours.

'Tom?'

His name sounded hesitant but laced with a concern that also triggered an automatic response in his exhausted state. His steps slowed and stopped. He turned.

'How could you?' His voice felt rusty. Broken, almost. 'How could you do that to me?'

He could see his pain reflected in the dark pool of her eyes. A man walked past with his dog and gave them both a curious stare.

'Not here.' Rebecca's touch on his arm was a plea. 'Come inside, Tom. Please.'

He was too tired to resist the touch. Nothing could be worse than what had already happened today but, if it was, he might as well get it over with.

And he wanted an answer to his question. So he wouldn't spend the rest of his life with it echoing in his head. And his heart.

How could you?

CHAPTER NINE

IT WAS WORSE than she feared.

Having forced herself to give her attention to representing a hospital that needed to stay exactly where it was to keep providing the superlative care that young transplant patients deserved, Rebecca had spent the rest of the picnic event and the long tidy-up afterwards worried about Thomas.

Where he was and what he was thinking. How much he might hate her for what had—unintentionally—happened when he'd been introduced to a recipient of one of Gwen's organs.

To find him virtually on her doorstep when she'd finally been able to make her way home had been astonishing. To see the sheer exhaustion in his body language and the anger in his eyes had been frightening. He'd been pushed well past any safety barriers he'd built up over the last few years. And he was blaming her?

At least he'd agreed to come inside. He would be facing ghosts that he'd done his best to avoid but maybe today had shown him that you couldn't avoid them. They would always be there so you had to accept them and, when you did, you didn't have to fear them so much. He was facing some of the grief he'd never processed. Perhaps this was the first step he needed to take to finally do that?

She'd never imagined him ever being here again. If she'd thought about it, she would have decided that it was the last thing *she* would ever want.

But here they were. And, who knew? Talking now might turn out to be the most honest conversation they would ever have.

Thomas said nothing as he followed Rebecca through the front door and down the tiny hallway. She saw him turn his head as they passed the two rooms on either side, one of which had been Gwen's bedroom and was now her office.

The hallway led into the living room where the old couch was still in exactly the same place but she didn't stop there. She took him through to the kitchen and busied herself putting on the kettle and lifting the teapot down from its shelf. Thomas sank down onto one of the two chairs at the small table by the window that looked out onto the shared garden.

The garden where Gwen had taken her first steps…

He said nothing until Rebecca placed a steaming mug of tea in front of him.

'I don't understand. I can't begin to understand why you did any of this.'

Rebecca sat on the other chair. They were close enough to touch but it felt like they were a million miles apart. 'Any of what?'

'The job you do. Having to spend so much time with families who've been destroyed. How you keep it in your life every single day.'

'It *is* in our lives every single day,' she said softly. 'Isn't it?'

'I don't obsess over it,' Thomas said. 'I don't go

looking for ways to make it harder. How could you have gone looking to find out who…who was out there…who was still alive because we lost our daughter?'

'I didn't go looking,' Rebecca told him. 'What I did do was to make myself known to the transplant association. I said I'd like to know if they were ever contacted by any of the recipients in the future because I thought it would help me to know that we hadn't made that decision for nothing. That there were lives that had been changed for the better. And…and they gave me a letter that Ava's mother had written more than a year before. It was waiting in the files, in case I ever asked for information. I've still got it, if you'd like to read it. It was addressed to both parents of their donor.'

She could see how painful it was for Thomas to swallow by the jerky movement of the muscles of his neck. He didn't say anything.

'Some of the words are blurry,' she added. 'Jude must have been crying when she wrote it. She wanted us to know that we'd given them a miracle. That they thought of us as part of their family and always would. That they would feel blessed if they could ever get a chance to thank us in person.' Rebecca swiped away the tears that were trickling from her eyes. 'I thought about it for a long, long time but I decided I wanted to meet her. Just Jude. Another mother who'd gone through the agony of facing the loss of her child.'

'But you didn't stop at that, did you?'

'No. The decision to meet Ava took a long time, too, and I was terrified about how I would feel. I cried all the way home. Most of that night, as well. But then I found that it had helped. That there was peace in knowing that we'd done the right thing. That a gorgeous kid like Ava has another chance at life. It really helped.'

'It's not helping me,' Thomas muttered.

'Not yet. But I think it will.'

'What makes you think you know how I feel?' Anger tipped each word, making them as sharp as arrows.

'I don't,' Rebecca admitted. 'But I want to help.'

'By throwing something like that at me? Without even warning me that it was a possibility?'

'That's not fair. I didn't know you were going to be there. We're only just getting to know each other again. Why would I have told you something that I knew you weren't ready to hear? Something that would push you away? I'm sorry it happened like that but…but I'm not sorry I'm part of Ava's life.'

'I don't want to be.'

'You don't have to be.' But, perhaps, even considering that possibility would help him process some more of that grief that he'd just shut away and tried to ignore. The grief that was keeping his life even more stuck than her own?

Their mugs of tea were cold. With a sigh, Rebecca got up and opened the fridge. She took out a bottle of wine and Thomas didn't protest when she put a glass in front of him. The only sound to break the silence for a long while was glass against wood as they picked up and put down their drinks.

It was Rebecca that broke the silence.

'It happened to both of us, Tom,' she said quietly. 'And it was the worst thing that could have ever happened. Nothing's going to change that but it doesn't wipe out the good stuff.'

'What *good* stuff?'

'How much we loved each other. How much we loved our daughter. We were good parents, Tom. We're good people.'

'*Were* we?' Thomas drained his glass. 'Why didn't we keep her safe, then?'

'We weren't even there.'

'Exactly.' Thomas reached for the bottle and refilled his glass. 'We were so wrapped up in our precious careers. Paying other people to look after our kid. If one of us had stayed at home, it wouldn't have happened.'

Rebecca caught her breath. 'One of us? You mean *me*? Are you saying *I* was a *bad* mother?'

His head shake was sharp. 'No. I could have been at home. Or we could have taken turns.'

'What happened was *not* our fault. It could have happened anywhere. We *could* have been there. On a Sunday afternoon when we were

going to the zoo, maybe. It was a freak accident, Tom. The footpath is supposed to be a safe
place to walk. For anyone, including a class out-
ing from nursery school. Nobody expects a car
to go out of control and hit people who are on a
footpath.'

'Oh… God…' Thomas covered his eyes with
his hand. 'It feels like it happened yesterday.'

Rebecca's chair scraped on the floorboards as
she moved it closer. Close enough for her to be
able to wrap her arms around Thomas and hold
him until the shaking and the tears subsided.

She was crying, too. And at some point Thomas
began holding her as much as she was holding
him. The daylight was rapidly fading from the
room but neither of them thought to move and
turn on a light. When they finally unwrapped
their arms enough to pull back and see each other's face, it felt like the middle of the night. The
way it used to sometimes, when they were in bed
together. Naked and vulnerable but…but safe, as
well, because they were with each other.

How could she have been so convinced that

Thomas could never be a part of her life again? Doubts were being washed away by a flood of remembered feelings. Of that safety. That love…

They were overwhelming. She couldn't stop the whispered words leaving her lips.

'I still love you, Tom. I've missed you *so* much…'

It was so easy to lean closer again and touch her lips against his. Maybe he'd moved at the same time because the pressure was much greater than she'd expected it to be. Nothing like that gentle kiss of comfort they had shared that night after that dance.

This kiss had an almost desperate edge that was like trying to catch hold of something precious that had been lost and was fleetingly in sight again. Or maybe it was the aftermath of a deep, shared grief that was begging for an affirmation of life.

Of love…

Whatever was behind it only got more powerful as lips and then tongues traced such well-remembered patterns. As hands moved to touch skin beneath clothes.

It was Thomas who stood up first, drawing Rebecca to her feet.

It was Rebecca who kept hold of his hand and led him through the darkness to the bedroom.

Had Thomas really believed that today would be one he never wanted to remember?

How wrong could he have been?

But the last thing he could have imagined happening was to be here, like this. In his old bed.

Cradling the woman he had always loved in his arms as she slept in the aftermath of such a passionate physical reconnection.

And how could something like sex have seemed so right when it had come from such a gruelling emotional roller-coaster that had been fuelled by grief and anger and…and bone-deep loneliness?

He adjusted the weight of Rebecca's head on his arm and she sighed in her sleep. Her breath was a warm puff against the skin of his chest.

This felt right.

Walking for all those hours yesterday hadn't dealt with any of those heart-wrenching emotions but it seemed that making love to Rebecca had done more than he could have believed was possible.

Because it had been making love and not simply sex. And for the first time since that terrible accident, Thomas felt at peace.

Exhausted, too, of course. And unsure enough of what his future looked like now to be unable to allow sleep to claim him just yet but he was happy just to be here. To feel as if a small piece of his shattered world had just been put back together.

No. Not a small piece.

The biggest part of it, maybe.

Was that being disloyal to Gwen's memory? From the moment of her birth, she had been the sun that their lives revolved around. The bonus that made them a family instead of a couple. The living promise of the future they'd both dreamed of.

Thomas found himself listening to the silence of the apartment around them. Could he hear the echo of childish laughter? The patter of small feet running across the floorboards?

They hadn't even thought of pulling the blinds down on the windows when they'd come into this room so there were shards of light from the streetlamp on the road above. If he turned his head just a little, Thomas could see the framed photographs on Rebecca's bedside table and he stared at them for the longest time.

There were three photographs.

One of them was the first photograph of Gwen ever taken. She was lying in Rebecca's arms, only minutes after her birth and mother and baby were gazing at each other as if nothing so incredible had ever happened in the world.

Another was the photograph of them beside the bronze gorilla at the zoo when both the girls in his life had been laughing up at him and he had the grin of the happiest man in the world.

And the last photograph had been taken years before they became a family. Before Gwen had even been a possibility. Newly in love, on a weekend away, he and Rebecca had gone into one of those automatic photo booths. He could remember the strip of black-and-white images, most of which had been them making silly faces. But then they'd kissed.

The tiny photo Rebecca had chosen to put into a heart-shaped frame had been the moment they'd broken that kiss. When their lips were only just apart and they were looking at each other as if there could never be anyone else on the planet who could make them feel like this.

Something tightened in his chest and squeezed so hard that Thomas couldn't take a breath.

Rebecca had been right.

There *was* good stuff that could never be wiped out.

Like how much they had loved each other and how happy they had been together.

He turned away from the photographs to press a gentle kiss to Rebecca's head.

'I love you, too,' he whispered. 'I'm sorry I forgot how much.'

And then he listened again. Yes. He could hear those echoes. And it did make him feel sad but sadness wasn't the only thing he was aware of. He could remember the love and the laughter. The *good* stuff.

The kind of stuff that another little girl's parents were being blessed with when they'd faced the prospect of losing it for ever. A little girl with long blonde braids and blue eyes.

That unexpected flush of pride returned.

Not that he was going to let the worst of those memories surface. It was enough to register this new perspective for just a heartbeat. They *had* done the right thing in making that agonising decision that day. He was proud of it.

Proud of them both.

Thomas let his eyes drift shut, his cheek resting against the softness of Rebecca's hair. In the final moment before he fell deeply asleep, he turned his head a fraction to press another soft kiss to her forehead.

It felt like far more than the start of a new week the next morning.

It felt like the start of a new life.

But new born was also fragile and Rebecca wasn't going to take anything for granted. Not even when their lovemaking at dawn had been so heartbreakingly tender. Something they had both chosen to do that hadn't been prompted by any need for release in the wake of being put through an emotional wringer.

Thomas didn't stay for breakfast.

'I need to get home and changed,' he said. 'What would people think if I turned up to work with you, looking like I'd slept under a hedge for a week?'

'They might think that it was the best news ever.' Rebecca followed him to the door and smiled up at him, her heart too full of joy to hold the words back. 'That Dr Wolfe and Dr Scott had found each other again.'

Thomas was smiling, too. 'Have we, Becca? Have we found each other again?'

The full glow of this reborn connection might be fragile but fragile things needed nurturing, didn't they?

'I hope so.' She reached up to touch his face. 'I don't think I ever stopped loving you, Tom.'

He bent to kiss her. A soft touch that clung for a heartbeat and then another.

'Same,' he whispered. 'But I still need to change my clothes.'

Rebecca watched him climb the steps and let herself dream for a moment. Maybe, soon, his clothes would be back where they belonged— in their wardrobe. And Thomas would be back where he belonged, too.

With her.

The sound of her mobile phone ringing brought her back to the present.

'Dr Scott? Rebecca?'

'Speaking.'

'It's Louise Walker. I'm sorry to ring you so early but… I've been awake all night.'

'That's fine, Louise. How can I help?'

'We decided. Last night. We talked about it with the whole family and we all feel the same way…'

Rebecca's heart squeezed at the pain in the

young mother's voice. It didn't matter what the decision was, it had been hard won and she was happy that the whole family was in agreement. Louise couldn't see her nodding, or that she had closed her eyes as she waited out the silence as Louise fought for control of her voice.

'We're ready,' she whispered. 'We want Ryan to be a donor.'

CHAPTER TEN

THE NEEDLES OF hot water in his shower landed on skin that felt oddly raw.

As a young boy, Thomas Wolfe had been fascinated by arthropods—invertebrate creatures who had to shed their exoskeleton because it restricted growth—like grasshoppers and stick insects.

He felt like a human version.

The emotional shock of confronting the very real evidence that parts of his own daughter still existed had cracked the shell he'd been inside for years. Talking to Rebecca had painfully peeled more of that shell away. Being touched and touching with so much love had been the rebirth of the man who'd been hidden. The man he used to be.

Hermit crabs. They were another creature that could emerge from their old shell and start again and he'd definitely been a hermit in an emotional sense.

Was that part of his life over?

Could he start again, with Rebecca by his side?

How miraculous would that be?

The way the water stung was a warning to be careful, however, not to rush anything. Arthropods were at their most vulnerable when newly emerged. He was sure he remembered a statistic that moulting was responsible for something like eighty to ninety per cent of arthropod deaths. They needed time for their new shells to harden.

He needed time, too.

Arriving at Paddington's for the start of the new working week made things feel more normal and boosted his confidence.

There was no need to rush anything. Safety—for both himself and Rebecca—was paramount.

There was a television crew in the area near the main reception desk. Annette, one of the senior members of the team that staffed the desk, waved at Thomas.

'Dr Wolfe? I was just telling these visitors that

you're just the person who might be able to answer this query.'

'What's that?' Thomas frowned, trying to remember where he'd seen the perfectly groomed blonde woman who was smiling as he approached. Oh, yes…she'd been the person interviewing Rebecca at the Teddy Bears' Picnic yesterday.

Good grief! With all that had happened since, it felt like a very long time ago.

'I'm Angela Marton,' she introduced herself. 'We're hoping to film a feature on a child that's waiting for a transplant. There was such an overwhelmingly positive response to our coverage from the picnic yesterday. We thought a more in-depth story would help raise awareness of the need for donors. And Paddington's needs all the good publicity it can get at the moment, doesn't it?'

'I can't give permission for something like that,' Thomas said. 'You'll have to speak to our CEO—Dr Bradley—about that.'

'Where is it that you work?'

'I'm in Cardiology.'

'Oh…' Angela's eyes lit up. 'You don't happen to have someone waiting for a heart transplant, do you? A family who might be prepared to share their story?'

'I'm afraid our patient information is completely confidential.'

'Mmm… Of course it is. I totally respect that.'

The look in her eyes suggested otherwise. People were always keen to talk if it gave them a moment of fame, weren't they? Penelope Craig was well-known around Paddington's. Who knew whether an orderly or clerk or even a kitchen hand had overheard things that they could share?

The need to protect Penny and her family from a possibly unwelcome intrusion in their lives made Thomas excuse himself. Hopefully, they could send Penny home today and he wouldn't feel so responsible if their privacy was invaded. His pager sounded at the same time, which added weight to his comment that he was needed elsewhere.

The pager message was to find a phone to accept an external phone call from Dr Rebecca Scott. Thomas felt a beat of excitement as Annette handed him a phone he could use. He couldn't wait to hear Rebecca's voice. He wanted to *see* her again, in fact—the sooner, the better.

It was more than hope that this new beginning was going to take them back to where they'd once been.

In love.

Married.

With a shared dream of a future together...

It was the strength of the *wanting* that made him so aware of how soft this new shell of his still was.

To want something this much and not achieve it had the potential to destroy him all over again. And there would be no coming back from going through that a second time.

He distracted himself from that fear by focusing on a much more mundane detail. It was high time they had each other's mobile numbers, wasn't it? Using a formal contact process like this was not appropriate for anything personal.

Except it wasn't anything personal that Rebecca wanted to talk to him about.

'I'm just on my way into work,' she said. 'I've had a call from the parents of a little boy that was declared brain-dead a few days ago and they've agreed to let him become a donor. I'll get onto the matching processes as soon as I get in. It's just possible that he could be a match for Penny so I thought I'd better give you a heads-up. It would be a shame to discharge her and then bring her straight back in.'

Thomas eyed Angela and her crew, who were now standing near an elevator looking for directions towards Dr Bradley's office. He lowered his voice, anyway.

'How far away is the donor? Will you have to travel for the retrieval?'

'No.' Rebecca's voice was quiet. 'He's in our own intensive care unit.'

'Oh…' Thomas blinked, taken aback. He remembered a snatch of conversation he'd overheard that night at the Frog and Peach, when Rebecca had been talking to Alistair North. He didn't want to know any more, though—like the name or age of this boy. In fact, hadn't he heard something not so long ago? About one of the children who'd been injured so badly in the school fire?

He didn't allow any additional information of who it might be to surface because it felt too close to home. Too personal. Keeping things as anonymous as possible was the sensible way to handle this.

'Fine,' he said then. 'Thanks for the heads-up. I'll keep things on hold until we know more and then I can either discharge her or initiate the final work-up.'

'Cool, thanks. I'll let you know as soon as possible.'

'Great. And, Becca...?'

Her tone changed, becoming suddenly softer and warmer. He could imagine her lips curving into a private smile. 'Yes?'

'Thanks for last night. For...everything.'

There was a moment's silence. 'I'll see you

soon,' Rebecca said, and it sounded like a promise. 'And, Tom?'

'Yes?'

'Maybe you can give me your mobile number?'

His mouth curled into a smile of his own. 'I've got your number from this call. I'll text you mine.'

Penelope was wearing her pink tutu skirt. She also had a diamante, princess tiara on the top of her head. She was sitting, cross-legged, on the covers of her bed, her eyes glued to the latest adventures of the Ballerina Bears. Her toys and games and art supplies were all packed into suitcases in a corner of the room but her parents didn't look happy about any of it.

They looked totally stunned.

'But...' Julia's bottom lip trembled. 'But we were going to take her home today. That's why she's wearing her crown. She's going to be a princess for the day and we've got her carriage waiting. And she's looking so *well...*'

Peter took hold of her hand. 'But this is what we've been waiting for, hon. This could mean years and years of her being well.' His voice cracked and he cleared his throat, shifting his gaze from his wife to the two doctors in front of them.

'Are you sure? This is an exact match?'

'As close as we could hope for.' Rebecca smiled. 'We need to do another blood test on Penny. It's the final comparison of the donor's blood cells and Penny's blood serum to make sure that she hasn't created any new antibodies that might attack the donated organ. It's very unlikely, but we need to check.'

'And if it's okay?' Julia's eyes were wide and terrified. 'When…?'

'The sooner, the better,' Thomas said. 'We've got a hold on a theatre for about two this afternoon.'

Julia's head swivelled to look at her daughter. Penny didn't notice because she was staring at her hands, trying to follow the direction her beloved bears were giving each other.

'You use your thumb and your middle finger,'

Sapphire was telling her friends. 'Like you're holding a tiny magic stone…'

Julia tried to hold back her tears. It was her loud sniff that attracted Penny's attention.

'What's the matter, Mummy?'

'Nothing, darling. I'm…happy, that's all.'

'Because we're going home?'

Thomas smiled. 'What is it that you want most of all, Penny?'

'To be a ballerina.' The little girl's smile stretched from ear to ear.

'And what is it that you need so that you *can* be a ballerina?'

'A new heart.' Her tone was matter-of-fact. As if it was a solution as simple as getting a new pair of shoes.

It was Peter who went close enough to the bed to stroke Penny's head. 'What would you say if we told you that you might be able to get that new heart today?'

Penny shook her head. 'But we're going home, today, Daddy. Can we do it tomorrow?'

Then she looked slowly around the room and

the television programme was forgotten as the magnitude of what was going on around her sank in. The smile everybody associated with this brave little girl wobbled and her voice was very small.

'Do I have to have another operation?'

'Just one.' Rebecca sat on the chair beside Penny's bed and took a small hand in hers. 'And then we hope there won't be any more. Maybe ever...'

'And the new heart will make me better?'

Rebecca nodded and smiled. 'That's the plan, sweetheart.'

'And I can go back to school?'

'Yes.'

'And I can have ballet lessons?'

'Yes.' It was Julia who answered this time. 'Of course you can.'

Thomas watched the look that passed between Penny's parents as they gripped each other's hands. He could see the mix of fear and hope and he could feel it himself. The protective shield he'd kept between himself and his patients and their families just didn't seem to be there any more.

He looked back at Penny, who was smiling at Rebecca now.

'Okay, I guess it's okay if I don't go home today.'

And then Thomas let his gaze rest on Rebecca's face. That smile that he loved so much. That look she was giving Penny that told the little girl she was the most important person in the world right now. He could feel her determination that she was going to give Penny and her family what they wanted so desperately.

And he could feel his own love for Rebecca that was a big part of the emotional mix in this room. He wanted a successful outcome as much as anybody else here.

He could feel everything with such clarity, it was painful.

Because of his new, soft shell?

He'd forgotten what this felt like. Hope. The anticipation of something so joyful, it made the world look like a different place.

A much better place than he'd been living in for such a long time.

There was nothing more for him to do here. Penelope Craig was Rebecca's patient now, and would be until she was discharged with her new heart to return to the care of her cardiologist. He wanted to be there, though. He wanted to be in the gallery to watch the surgery. To let Rebecca know that she had his complete support and to meet her gaze if she chose to look up and seek encouragement. The way he had when the first surgery had been done on this very child.

How appropriate would it be for him to be there again, now, in what could be the definitive surgery that could give her many years of life? That he could celebrate their new connection by repeating history and letting her know that he believed in her.

That he—once again—believed in *them*?

He also wanted to be by her side when she went to tell Julia and Peter how well it had all gone.

It would be a long surgery. He needed to clear everything else on his agenda today to put the time aside.

* * *

The urgent call to the intensive care unit came shortly after the message from Rebecca that said the green light had been given to the suitability of the donor heart and its intended recipient. Penelope Craig was now in the final stages of her pre-theatre preparation.

The patient Thomas had been called to see was a six-month-old baby who'd been admitted and rushed to intensive care in a life-threatening condition. He arrived to see an alarmingly fast trace on the ECG monitor and a baby with a bulging fontanelle who was struggling to breathe and going blue. The baby's terrified mother was standing to one side with a nurse.

'Oxygen saturation is improving with the nasal cannula,' he was told. 'Up from eighty-four per cent on room air.'

Thomas looked at the ECG printout he was handed. 'Looks like a supraventricular tachycardia. Other vitals?'

'Respiratory rate of sixty-five, blood pressure

is eighty on fifty and she's febrile at thirty-nine point four degrees.'

'Deep tendon reflexes?'

'Brisk.'

'We could be looking at meningoencephalitis, then. Or meningitis.'

'A spinal tap is next on our list. But we need to get this tachycardia under control.'

'I agree.' The heart rate was far too rapid to be allowing enough oxygen to circulate and it was a very unstable situation. Thomas had his fingers on the baby's arm. 'I've got a palpable peripheral pulse. Let's try some IV adenosine with a two-syringe rapid push. If that doesn't help, we'll go for a synchronised cardioversion.'

The drug therapy was enough to slow the heart rate to an acceptable level. Thomas stayed with the baby a little longer, as treatment to bring down her fever and improve oxygen levels was started. He wrote up lab forms to check electrolyte levels that could well need correction to prevent further disruptions to the heart rhythm.

And then he left, after a glance at his watch told

him that Penny would be heading for the operating theatre within an hour or so. So would the donor of her heart. They would be in side-by-side theatres. Other theatres may also have been cleared and there could very well be a retrieval team from another transplant centre waiting to rush precious organs to other children in desperate need.

It was no real surprise, then, to see Rebecca up here.

What shocked him was that she had her arm around another woman who was sobbing quietly, her head on Rebecca's shoulder.

A chill ran down his spine at the realisation that this had to be the mother of the donor child.

He had to walk past them. Despite every ounce of willpower he could summon, Thomas couldn't prevent his head turning. The door to the room was open. His glance only grazed the scene within but it was instantly seared into his memory bank.

A small boy, so still on the bed, his head bandaged and a hand lying, palm upwards as though it had just been released from being held.

His father sitting beside him, his head in his hands and his shoulders shaking.

Rebecca didn't even see him going past, she was so focused on the woman beside her.

'There's still time,' he heard her murmur. 'Go and be with Ryan. And with Peter. He needs you. You need each other…'

The chill didn't stop when it reached the end of Thomas's spine. It seemed to be spreading to every cell in his body.

He was that father.

He could feel the utter desolation of knowing that, very soon, the final goodbye would have to happen. That they would walk beside the bed that their child was lying on until they got as close as they were allowed to Theatre. That they were about to lose even the appearance of life that the intensive care technology could provide.

He could feel his world crumbling around him all over again.

And Rebecca's words unleashed another cascade of terrible memories.

You need each other…

He hadn't been there for her when she'd needed him. Not in any meaningful way. He'd started to pull himself into his shell from the moment they'd taken Gwen further along that corridor that led to the operating theatre and he'd just made himself more and more unavailable.

Not because he'd *wanted* to. Hurting the woman he loved so much was the last thing he would have ever chosen to do. He just hadn't been able to survive any other way.

And who was to say he wouldn't do it again?

Even now, as he walked away from the paediatric intensive care unit, Thomas could feel himself frantically looking for some mental building materials, desperate to try and resurrect at least enough of a barrier to protect himself from this wash of unbearable emotion that seeing the donor's family had induced.

No, it wasn't just an anonymous donor any more.

His name was Ryan, and Thomas clearly remembered having heard the story. He was the little boy who'd gone to school, just like he would have on any other ordinary day. But the unthinkable had happened and he'd been badly injured in that fire at his school.

And he had parents who loved him as much as he and Rebecca had loved their little Gwen.

Thomas took the stairs. He couldn't stand next to anyone waiting for an elevator right now, let alone have the doors slide shut to confine him.

He needed space. A private place to somehow deal with this onslaught of memories that had been buried so deeply he'd thought he was safe from feeling like this again. So he headed up the stairs, instead of down. All the way to the top of the building and through the door that led to the helipad. Empty at the moment, with nothing more than the most amazing view of central London on display. He walked to the furthest corner he could find and stood there, staring at familiar landmarks.

Like the green spaces of the parks and the bump of Primrose Hill where he'd held Rebecca in his arms for the first time since they'd parted and this whole cascade of reconnection had begun. He could see the rooftop and signage of the Frog and Peach over the road where he'd danced with her that night. He could even make out the wrought-iron fences further along the road that marked the spot where he'd kissed her.

He couldn't do it, he realised.

He couldn't allow even a possibility of hurting Rebecca all over again.

Going to the Teddy Bears' Picnic yesterday had been a mistake but it paled in comparison to what had happened between them last night.

It couldn't happen again.

He wasn't going to allow Rebecca to risk her future happiness by being with him. He was the one who couldn't handle these memories.

He was the one who was really stuck. So he was the one who had to set her free to find a new future.

With someone else.

But how—and when—could he tell her that?

Maybe very soon, he thought as his mobile phone began to ring and he saw the name 'Becca' on the screen.

He swiped to answer the call but he didn't get time for any kind of greeting.

'Tom? Where are you?' Rebecca sounded alarmed.

'What's wrong?'

'It's Penny… She's gone missing…'

CHAPTER ELEVEN

'WHAT DO YOU MEAN—gone missing?'

'We can't find her. I came up to see her and check that everything was ready for her to go to Theatre and she's not in her room. She's nowhere in the ward.'

Thomas had already turned away from the view and from any thoughts remotely personal. His stride, as he headed back to the door leading to the stairwell, was verging on a run.

'I don't understand. How could she have gone anywhere? Who was with her?'

'That's just it. No one.'

'*What?*' Thomas hit the button to release the automatic door with the flat of his hand.

'It was only for a minute or two, apparently. Peter had gone to Reception to meet Penny's grandparents. Julia had dashed to the loo and

Rosie responded to an alarm that signalled an emergency in the treatment room. She wasn't needed, in the end, and went straight back but Penny had disappeared. Rosie thought she'd gone to find her mum in the loo but Julia hadn't seen her.'

'She can't be far away. She's probably visiting one of her friends.' Thomas was taking the stairs, two at a time.

'She's not in the ward. We've checked. Everybody's looking for her. Rosie's beside herself. She thinks it's her fault but it was a cardiac arrest alarm and she said Penny promised to stay in bed.'

'Have you called Security?'

'Yes. They've been all over it for the last ten minutes. Nobody's seen her.'

Maybe Thomas hadn't completely banished personal thoughts. Penelope Craig was still his patient, even though her care was to be in Rebecca's hands for the next little while.

He could understand why Rosie was feeling

so bad but Penny's safety was ultimately *his* responsibility.

Like keeping her family safe from the intrusion of that television crew had been, especially today of all days.

To see Angela and her camera and sound people milling around the space near the stairs as he exited on the floor of the cardiology ward was like a slap in the face. The lens of the camera was like a giant eye, swivelling to point straight at him as his presence was noted.

'Dr Wolfe? Is it true that a little girl's gone missing? One that was about to have a heart transplant?'

'No comment.' Thomas pushed past the reporter. How on earth had the news been leaked so quickly?

How hard should it have been to have stopped these strangers finding out anything about Penny? It felt like a personal failure.

And there was a list of other personal failures that it could be added to.

Like not having this special patient in the place

that she was supposed to be in order to receive her life-saving surgery.

Like not having been in the right place at the right time to keep his own daughter safe.

And, above all, like not having been able to keep his marriage safe.

He hadn't even heard the last question Angela was calling after him but he raised his hand in a silent 'no comment' gesture. He could see Rebecca in the ward corridor through the double doors. She was amongst a cluster of people that included Penny's parents and grandparents and a man he recognised as Jim, the head of Paddington's security team. Rosie was also there, her face pale and desperately worried.

And, no matter what the odds had been for Penny surviving the surgeries and setbacks she'd already had in her short life, he'd never seen Julia Craig looking this terrified.

'She's probably just found a place to hide,' Jim was saying as Thomas joined the group. 'I expect she was frightened about having to go to Theatre again. We'll find her, Mrs Craig. Please try not to worry too much.'

Julia shook her head. 'She wouldn't just run away—it's not like her at all. And she said she'd stay in bed, didn't she?'

Rosie nodded. 'I was gone such a short time, Julia. I'm so sorry…'

'It's not your fault. I would have left her to go to the loo if you hadn't been there. I've done that a million times.'

'She hasn't been *able* to run anywhere before this,' Peter put in. 'Because she's been too sick. But now… Who knows how far she could have gone?'

'Somebody will have seen her,' Jim said. 'How many little girls do we see wearing a pink tutu and a princess crown? I've got my men every-where. We're combing the entire hospital.'

'But what if she isn't in the hospital any more?' Julia whispered. 'What if someone's…?' Her breath hitched. 'What if someone's *taken* her?'

'I've got someone reviewing CCTV footage right now. And we've started with the main doors. We've also called in the police.' He turned towards Rebecca. 'How long have we got? When does her surgery have to happen by?'

'We've got a bit of time,' Rebecca answered. 'But that's not the point. What matters is *finding* Penny—as soon as we possibly can.' She ran her hand over her head. 'I can't just wait here. I'm going to start looking myself.'

Her gaze snagged Thomas's as she turned away and his own concern ramped up into real alarm as he saw the fear in her eyes.

Was it at all possible that someone *had* taken Penny? Had she wandered far enough away from the ward for some random predator to spot an opportunity?

It was so unlikely that he would have dismissed the notion as ridiculous up until now.

But, a long time ago, he would have said the same thing about a random car going out of control and mounting a footpath, wouldn't he?

Nothing was impossible, however horrible it might be.

And the fear in Rebecca's eyes was impossible to ignore. As much as he knew he couldn't allow her to depend on him for what she needed, he had to help.

'I'll come with you,' he said.

'We'll try the playground again,' Peter said. 'In case she's come back.'

'And I'll check under every bed,' Rosie added. 'And in every cupboard. She's *got* to be somewhere.'

Jim looked up, ending a call he'd been taking on his phone.

'CCTV from every exit has been checked. There's no sign of her having been taken anywhere and we've got every door covered by security now. She's here. *Somewhere...*'

They started in the wards closest to Cardiology and talked to everybody they encountered.

'Have you seen a little girl? Wearing a pink tutu?'

'No...sorry... We'll keep an eye out.'

'Do you mind if we have a look in the storeroom? She could be trying to hide.'

She was such a little thing, Rebecca thought, moving a laundry bag in its wheeled frame to one side in that storeroom. She'd be able to squeeze into the smallest place.

'I don't understand why she wanted to run away,' she said to Thomas. 'It's not as if this is her first operation. I'm sure I didn't make it sound scary.'

'I'm sure you didn't,' he agreed. 'But who knows what might make a six-year-old kid feel nervous?'

A six-year-old kid?

Just another child?

Thomas didn't seem to be feeling anything like the level of anxiety gripping Rebecca.

'This is *Penny* we're talking about, Tom.'

'Mmm… Maybe the wards are the wrong place to be looking. I wonder if anybody's checked an outpatient area like Physiotherapy. Or the X-ray department?'

He was already walking away from her and Rebecca stared at his back. It felt like she was being accompanied in this search by a member of the security team. Someone who hadn't known Penny for her entire life and had no personal involvement in her case.

The chill hit her like a bucket of icy water.

Thomas was running away again. Hiding behind those self-protective barriers. Pretending he wasn't involved so he could distance himself from the discomfort of anxiety—or worse. Because he felt guilty? Okay, Penny was his patient but it was ridiculous to assume responsibility for something that had happened when he was nowhere near her. When other people had accepted that mantle of responsibility.

That hadn't stopped him from blaming himself over Gwen's death, though, had it?

It hadn't stopped him believing he had failed as a father.

But how could he do this, when they'd been so close again only last night? When they'd talked about exactly how it *hadn't* been his fault?

Fear stepped in then. How could she have allowed herself to resurrect and sink into those feelings for Thomas? To dream about a shared life again?

This was a tough moment in their professional lives but she needed his support and he was creating a distance that hurt. If they got together again, how long would it be before something important went wrong and she really needed him again?

She couldn't do this.

Because—maybe—she couldn't trust Thomas enough.

But now wasn't the time to think about any of that. Not only was Rebecca desperately worried about the state of mind of a patient she loved dearly, there was a clock ticking. Penny wasn't going to be the only recipient of one of Ryan's organs and there were retrieval teams already arriving at Paddington's. Ryan's surgery would be going ahead whatever happened. If Penny couldn't be found, his heart might have to go to the next person on the waiting list.

Minutes flashed past as they raced along corridors and into every space that might be accessible to a newly mobile little girl. Thirty minutes and then sixty.

Rebecca answered a phone call that informed her that there had still been no sighting of Penny. And then another that confirmed that Ryan would be on his way to Theatre very soon.

'We're running out of time,' she told Thomas as they waited for an elevator to get down to Reception. It had been someone in X-ray who'd thought they'd seen a girl in a pink dress in the toy shop.

Rebecca had to close her eyes tightly to hold back tears of despair.

Surely Thomas could see how upset she was? Just a touch on her arm or an encouraging word would be enough. Maybe even enough to dispel the horrible feeling that he was as distant now as he'd been when he'd first come back to Paddington's.

But he hadn't moved any closer when she opened her eyes as the lift doors slid open.

And he hadn't said a word.

A very pregnant woman, with long, glossy dark hair, stepped out of the lift. She stared at Thomas for a moment and then smiled as she obviously remembered who he was.

'It's Thomas, isn't it? We met in A&E the day of the school fire.'

'And don't I know you?' Rebecca said. 'You're a paramedic, aren't you? And you and Dominic were a big part of the early publicity in the campaign to save Paddington's?'

The woman nodded. 'Victoria,' she said. 'Victoria Christie—but soon to be MacBride. Dom's persuaded me to marry him.'

She was smiling, but the smile suddenly faded. 'I've just come in for an antenatal check,' she said. 'But what on earth's going on around here? There are police officers and reporters all over the place. Reception is crazy...'

Rebecca glanced at Thomas. 'Maybe the toyshop isn't the best place to check, then. If there are already so many people down there, someone would have spotted a little girl in a pink tutu.'

'A pink tutu?' Victoria's eyes widened. 'Are you talking about Penny?'

Thomas had been holding the lift doors open by

keeping his hand on them. A malfunction alarm began to sound.

'You know her?'

'I've transported her so often she's like a part of the family. And she's the only kid I know who would sleep in her tutu if she was allowed to.'

'She's gone missing,' Thomas said.

'And she's due in Theatre,' Rebecca added. 'We've got a heart available for her. A perfect match.'

'Oh, my God...' Victoria was looking horrified.

'We've got to go, but can you keep an eye out for her? I'm not sure if anyone's checked Ultra-sound or Maternity, yet.'

'Of course I will. I'd spot that tutu a mile off.'

'She's got a crown on today, as well.' Rebecca had to swallow past the lump in her throat. 'She's being a princess for the day.'

Victoria nodded, moved out of their way so they could get into the lift, but then swung back towards them.

'That reminds me of something. Have you checked the turret?'

'What?' Thomas put his hand back into the gap as the doors were closing and they opened again with a jerk.

'We were talking about the turret one day in the ambulance. The big one over Reception? I told her about how, when I was a kid, I'd always thought that a princess lived there but that, actually, it's only a dusty old storeroom full of ancient books and bits of paper.'

'I didn't even know you could get into it,' Rebecca said.

'You're not supposed to,' Victoria said. 'But there's a door. It looks like it's just a cupboard but then you find the staircase. I told Penny about that door. About the staircase…'

It was Thomas who caught Rebecca's gaze as the doors slid shut and the lift began to descend. She could see the hope in his eyes that maybe *this* was the breakthrough they'd been waiting for. A place that nobody would have thought to look because nobody even knew it was accessible?

The glance was unguarded only for the time it

took for Thomas to blink. And then he was staring straight ahead at the blank metal of the doors.

'Don't get your hopes up too much,' he murmured. 'It would be a miracle if she'd found that door and hadn't been spotted by someone in Reception.'

As Victoria had warned, the area around the main reception desk was crowded. They showed their official IDs to a police officer who was directing the general public towards a temporary information kiosk that had been set up outside the pharmacy.

The television reporter, Angela Marton, was speaking directly into a camera.

'From what we understand, a child—a small girl who is desperately in need of a new heart—has gone missing, only minutes before her surgery was due to take place.'

At least they hadn't revealed her name, Thomas thought. He put his hand up to shade the side of his face. Angela knew he was a cardiologist and she certainly knew that Rebecca was a transplant surgeon after interviewing her at the Teddy

Bears' Picnic. If she spotted either of them, they would have to fight their way through a media scrum to get where they needed to go.

But Angela seemed oblivious to any movement around her.

'This is what it's about, folks. This emergency situation—even more than the tragic fire at Westbourne Grove Primary School—is showing us what this hospital is all about. There isn't a single member of staff here who isn't searching for this little girl right now. Hoping that—any minute now—there will be an end to the dreadful worry her family is experiencing. Everybody cares... *so* much...'

The tiny break in her voice suggested that Angela cared as much as everybody else but Thomas knew that she would lead the pack that would snap at their heels if she sensed a new lead in the unexpected drama she was in the middle of. He tried to shield Rebecca with his body as he led them through the press of people and around the far end of the reception desk.

And there was the door. Inconspicuous enough

to be simply part of the wall and tucked far enough behind a rack of filing cabinets that it couldn't be seen from the other side of the reception desk. It wasn't impossible that nobody would have noticed a small girl going through this door. A glance behind him showed Thomas that nobody was watching them as he waited for Rebecca to slip through the gap and then followed her.

The attention of the film crew—and everybody else—had shifted to a group of uniformed people, one of whom was carrying an insulated box. It had to be a retrieval team from another hospital but Angela made a very different interpretation.

'Oh, my… Could that be the heart *arriving*?'

How long would Ryan's family be able to remain anonymous? It was a blessing that the assumption was being made that the heart was arriving from an anonymous donor somewhere else in the country but Thomas could still feel the tension ramping up sharply as he shut the door behind him. Ramping up as steeply as this narrow, spiral, wooden staircase. Round and round they went, leaving the chaos behind them. By the time they got to the top, it was so quiet, they could have been miles away from Paddington's. In a forgotten library, perhaps, with a circular room stuffed full of archived paperwork. The tension was still there but it felt different. As if the whole world was holding its breath.

Dust motes floated in the shafts of light coming through small, latticed windows. The floor was thick with dust, as well, but it had been disturbed. There were tracks in it.

'They look like adult-sized footprints.' Rebecca was whispering as if she, too, felt like she was in a library. 'Who could have been in here? I didn't even know it was possible.'

'Victoria did.'

'Mmm…' Rebecca was staring at the floor. 'Oh, my God, Tom! *Look*…'

And there it was.

A tiny footprint. Of a bare foot. He could even see the outline of where small toes had left their mark in the dust.

He took a step further into the round space.

And then another. Far enough to see past a tall stack of boxes. And there, curled up in the corner and fast asleep, was Penny. She had her head cushioned on one arm and her tiara was so lopsided it was almost covering one eye.

His overwhelming relief was echoed in Rebecca's gasp as she came past the tier of boxes but then it evaporated as fast as it had appeared.

Was Penny unconscious rather than asleep? Or *worse*… What if the device helping her heart to pump enough blood to the rest of her body had malfunctioned in some way because of an unexpected, additional stress—like climbing those steep stairs?

Thomas could feel the moment his own heart stopped because he felt the painful jolt as it started again with a jerk. He was crouching by then, his hand smoothing back one of Penny's braids to feel for a pulse in her neck.

A strong pulse…

Penny's eyes flickered open as she felt the touch. She looked up to see both Thomas and Rebecca bent over her and she smiled at them.

'Did you come up to see where the princess used to live, too?'

'We sure did.' It was hard to speak through the tightness in his throat. 'But it's time to go back now, sweetheart.'

'Okay.' Still smiling, Penny held up her arms. 'But I'm tired. Will you carry me?'

'Sure will,' Thomas managed.

'And I'm really, really *hungry*.'

'So you haven't had anything to eat? Or drink?'

His gaze caught Rebecca's as Penny's head was shaking a very definite and rather sad 'no.' At least that was another obstacle to getting her to Theatre that they wouldn't have to worry about.

By the time he'd scooped the little girl into his arms, she was sound asleep again. He stood up and turned and then stopped because he knew that Rebecca needed to touch this child herself— so that she could really believe that this crisis was over.

She had a tear rolling down the side of her nose and Thomas had to blink hard to hold back the prickle in his own eyes. And then Rebecca raised her gaze to his.

'You *do* care,' she whispered. 'As much as you ever did. You try and shut yourself away but it's not who you really are, is it?'

He could see more than relief in her dark eyes. He could see hope.

Hope that he couldn't allow to grow. But how could he destroy it?

'Of course I care,' he said quietly. 'Penny's my patient.'

'And she's fine. We'll get her to Theatre now. Everything's going to be all right.'

Thomas started moving towards the staircase. He would have to go very slowly and carefully. The stairs were narrow and steep.

It might not have been all right, he thought as they neared the bottom. *And it would have been my responsibility. My failure...*

'*What?*' Rebecca was ahead of him, her hand on the door handle, but her head turned sharply. She stopped moving.

Good grief! Had he spoken those thoughts aloud?

But Rebecca shook her head, as if she didn't believe what she might have heard. She turned the handle and, a moment later, he was stepping back into the real world of Paddington's. Penny stirred in his arms as she heard the exclamations of people around her that rapidly morphed from surprise to become a cheer. Undaunted by all the attention, she was beaming when she caught sight of her mother coming towards them and seemed oblivious to the flash of cameras around them.

'Make way, please.' Thomas held out his arm to clear a path towards the elevators. 'We don't have time for this...'

A hugely relieved Rosie was waiting in the ward to help give Penny a thorough check and get her ready for her trip to Theatre. Thomas and Rebecca worked together until they were both satisfied there was nothing to stop the surgery going ahead. Until the pre-surgery sedation had taken effect.

And, like she had after the VAD had been inserted, Rebecca touched her forefinger against her lips and then touched Penny's cheek to transfer the kiss.

'See you soon, pet,' she said softly. 'Sleep tight.'

It broke his heart how much he loved her for that tiny gesture that spoke of how much she cared, a promise that Penny wasn't going to be alone in what was to come.

It broke his heart to realise just how much he loved *her*...

And how much he was prepared to sacrifice to keep her safe.

Today's crisis could have had a very different ending and, even if it was irrational, he would still feel that at least part of it was a failure on his part.

He couldn't risk failing Rebecca again. Somehow, he had to tell her that but not yet. Not just before she was heading into Theatre for a surgery that was so crucial.

But he caught the glance she threw over her shoulder as she headed for the door and he knew she was picking up this new tension between them. He couldn't let her scrub up with that hanging over her, could he?

'Walk with me?'

'Sure.' Thomas walked by Rebecca's side towards the operating theatre locker rooms. He felt her glance at him more than once but it wasn't until they reached the storeroom that she finally said something.

'I can't leave it like this,' she said. 'I heard what you were muttering under your breath and I can't go into this surgery without saying something.'

Thomas had to lick his suddenly dry lips. 'About what?'

He got a loaded glance as a response to his being deliberately obtuse. Rebecca pulled supplies from the labelled shelves. A small-sized scrub tunic and pants, a cap and shoe covers.

'It wasn't your fault that Penny went missing,' she said. 'You've got to stop blaming yourself for things that you have no control over.'

This was it. A chance to say what he needed to say. Maybe Rebecca would understand.

'What about the things I should have had control over? Like being there for you when you needed me so much?'

Rebecca paused, the bundle of clean clothing in her arms. 'It takes two people to make a marriage work,' she said quietly. 'And maybe it takes two to make it fail. I didn't understand how bad it really was for you. Maybe I was too wrapped up in my own journey. I think I do now, though. When I had to go and speak to Ryan's parents that first time…' She took a slow inward breath. 'It was…really hard.'

Thomas was staring at the bundle of linen in Rebecca's arms but he was thinking of what he'd been holding such a short time ago. He could still feel the shape of Penny in his arms. How small and fragile she was. He could still feel the aftermath of that shock wave of thinking that she might not just be asleep. That they might have been too late. And that morphed into a different shock wave that he would never be able to erase from his memory.

Of arriving in the emergency department to

see Gwen when she'd been brought in after that terrible accident. Barely alive.

He'd certainly been too late, that time.

Rebecca could see that her words had triggered memories that Thomas was struggling with.

She needed to go. To get showered and changed and then start scrubbing in for the transplant surgery. Two lots of surgery, because she had to be the one to remove Ryan's heart to ensure the best possible outcome in reattaching the vital blood vessels.

And while she knew she could block out anything personal when she chose to focus completely on the tasks ahead of her, she couldn't leave Thomas looking so haunted. Not when it felt like she was losing him. She could feel everything they had found between them again—and everything they could find in the future—slipping away. Thomas was running again. Trying to find a safe place behind his barriers. She'd known it was happening during their search for Penny and it had rekindled all her doubts but then she'd seen the truth in his eyes when he'd been holding the little girl in his arms.

She'd seen the man she had always loved, who was capable of giving just as much love back, if only he could find a way past the burden of guilt he'd been carrying for so long. But the hope of that happening was also slipping away and what she said now might be her last chance of preventing that happening.

His next words confirmed her fears.

'I still feel like I failed Gwen,' he murmured. 'I was her daddy. I was supposed to keep her safe.'

'You were the *best* daddy.' Rebecca's voice was low but fierce. 'It wasn't your fault. There are no guarantees in life, Tom. We can only do our best. We can celebrate our successes and support each other if things don't go the way we hoped.'

'But I *didn't* support you. I can't risk that happening again.'

'So you're just going to give up? Run and hide?' The pain was sharpening her voice now.

'Maybe that's the only way I can keep *you* safe. To make sure I never hurt you again.'

Rebecca's breath came out in an incredulous huff. 'By staying away from me? Do you really think *that's* not going to hurt me?'

She couldn't deal with this now. Later, she would have to process the idea of losing Thomas all over again but, for now, it had to be pushed aside. Through the open door of the storeroom, she could see a bed being pushed along the corridor.

Ryan's bed.

The next few hours were going to test her to her limits. She not only had to use every skill she had to the best of her ability but she would have to ride that emotional roller-coaster from one end of the spectrum to the other.

She had to lose a tiny patient for ever.

And she had to give another one the gift of a new life.

She couldn't do it alone. She needed support and she needed it from someone who was trying to find a way to run away from her—and he believed that, by doing that, he was protecting her?

He couldn't be more wrong.

'Do one thing for me, Tom. Please?'

'What's that?'

'Be in the gallery. Not for this bit…' She would never ask him to do that—not when it would be like asking him to relive the final moments of his own child. 'Just for Penny's surgery?'

He'd been there for Penny's last operation. She could still remember how much confidence it had given her, knowing he was there simply to encourage her. To believe in her.

She needed him there for what would hopefully be Penny's final major surgery.

The bed and its entourage of medics were much closer now. Thomas turned his head and saw it.

Then he turned back to Rebecca. She could see so much pain in his eyes. But she could see something else, as well.

She could see how much he loved her…

'Yes.' His voice was no more than a whisper. 'I can do that. I'll be there.'

CHAPTER TWELVE

HE WASN'T RUNNING AWAY. But Thomas Wolfe *was* walking away. Temporarily.

He had no intention of not honouring his promise to be in the gallery for Penelope Craig's surgery but he couldn't hang around and wait knowing what was happening in Theatre Two right about now.

There were too many people here, as well. Theatre One was being prepared for Penny's surgery and Theatre Three had just been cleared for a child needing a new kidney. There were retrieval teams here for organs that would be rushed to other parts of the country adding to the congestion.

Thomas needed a space to centre himself. Maybe he needed to convince himself that he was doing the right thing.

That look in Rebecca's eyes when she'd asked him if he thought that removing himself from her personal life wouldn't hurt her...

He'd been so sure that it was the right thing to do.

So why did it feel so very wrong?

The rooftop could be a good place to go, although there might be helicopters waiting to transport those precious organs to their destinations as fast as possible. He needed to be careful which route he took to go anywhere, mind you. The media presence inside Paddington's right now was probably as big as it had been at any time during the whole campaign to save the hospital.

Bigger, even. They had a case that could highlight the importance of this beloved institution with the kind of drama people could lose themselves in. They already had the gripping opening of their story with Penny's disappearance and the frantic search. They had the tear-jerking reunion of the little girl with her parents and now the nail-biting tension of waiting to hear how the surgery had gone. They also knew who the two doctors were who were most involved in Penny's case and the last thing Thomas needed right now was to have a microphone or camera shoved in his face by Angela Marton and her colleagues.

His steps slowed as he neared the main doors that closed this floor of operating theatres and recovery areas from the foyer that contained the elevators and stairwells. Would there be cameras as close as right on the other side of those doors? He turned his head, even though he knew there was no other route to take. The only doors on either side of him led to a couple of small rooms that were used for things like meetings. Or for relatives that had been allowed to accompany a patient on the journey to Theatre but might not be able to cope with anything too clinical.

And that was when he saw them.

Ryan's parents.

They were sitting alone in one of the rooms.

Just sitting.

They were side by side but they weren't holding hands. They weren't talking to each other. At this precise moment, they weren't even looking at each other.

It was the sense of distance between them that hit Thomas so hard.

He knew they were both feeling utterly lost and that they each had to find their own way to start this most difficult of journeys but...

But if he could go back in time he would change the path *he* had taken.

He knew that this couple had probably asked for privacy after their final farewell of their son but something pushed Thomas to enter their space, uninvited.

To see if there was anything he could do to offer even the smallest amount of support.

They didn't seem to find his presence an intrusion. Maybe they needed something—anything—to give them a reference point in this bewildering new map of their lives. He pulled a chair out and perched on the edge of it, leaning forward as he spoke to them.

'This is the hardest part,' he told them. 'Taking the first steps into a life that's changed for ever.'

'No.' Peter Walker's voice was so raw it was painful to hear. 'The hardest part is knowing that I failed my son.'

It was tempting to break an unwritten rule and reveal something intensely personal but Thomas bit back the words. This wasn't about him.

Except, in a way, it was. Because he could hear himself saying the same thing. He could hear the echoes of it that had bounced around in his head for the last five years and he could see it inscribed in every brick of the walls he had built around his heart.

Where were those walls right now?

He could feel the pain of these young parents as acutely as if it was his own.

Because it still *was* his own?

But it was hearing someone who was the image of where he'd been five years ago saying his own destructive mantra aloud that made him realise how wrong it was.

'You *didn't* fail,' he told Peter. 'Neither of you did.'

Maybe it was the conviction in his tone that

made Julia lift her head from her hands and stare at him with the same expression as her husband. Waiting for him to say something else. Something that might give them a glimmer of comfort?

'You loved Ryan,' he said quietly. 'I know exactly how much you loved him because you're going through this right now and you'd only be doing this to give the gift of life to other children because you understand how much *their* parents love *them*.'

Both Julia and Peter had tears on their cheeks. They had turned to look at each other as Thomas was speaking and now they reached out and took each other's hands.

'You understand because that's how much you loved your little boy,' Thomas added. 'And, in the end, that's what really matters. He was loved. And he will always be loved because that kind of love never dies.'

It could be damaged, though, couldn't it?

Poisoned by self-blame. By running away and hiding. It could be lost even though it still existed.

'Help each other.' Thomas could hear the crack

in his own voice and he had to pause for a heart-beat to keep control. 'You've got tough times ahead but you'll get through them and—if you can help each other—you can be strong enough.'

It was time to leave them alone now. Thomas stood up but there was one more thing he needed to say.

'Believe that you were the best parents and that Ryan knew how much he was loved. And…' He had to swallow another lump in his throat. 'And be proud of what you're doing right now. Believe me, one day, you'll know it was exactly the right thing to do.'

Stepping out of the room, Thomas didn't even look at the doors that would have taken him away from this area.

He knew now, without the slightest shadow of doubt, that there was something else that was exactly the right thing to do.

And he was going to do it.

It was the last thing Rebecca Scott expected to see.

She surprised herself by even glancing up at the

gallery, in fact, because nobody came to watch this kind of surgery. It was hard on everybody and the atmosphere was sombre. Respectful and sad and there were several people in the extensive team in Theatre Two that were openly tearful.

But glance up at the gallery she did.

And there was Thomas.

Standing right behind the glass wall.

His posture told her that he was as sombre as any of them. Probably tearful himself as he grappled with memories that no parent should ever have to experience.

But he was here.

For her?

For himself?

No. As Rebecca stepped in to do her part of Ryan's last surgery, she knew that it was something bigger that had brought Thomas so close.

He was here for them both.

She couldn't tell if he was still in the gallery when she walked out of Theatre Two because she was blinded by tears that didn't stop falling until she'd finished scrubbing in again—this time for Penny's surgery.

Looking up at the gallery in Theatre One was the first thing she did as she entered a space that had a very different atmosphere.

This one was full of hope…

And that was what filled Rebecca as she looked up for a much longer moment this time, her lips curving with just a hint of a smile.

Thomas didn't seem to be smiling but it was hard to tell because he was touching his forefinger to his lips.

Then he touched the glass between them with that fingertip.

And Rebecca could feel that fairy kiss just as surely as if it had been his lips touching her skin. Telling her how much he cared and that she wasn't alone…

From the instant she looked away, her focus was completely on her work. This was the ultimate in the specialty she had chosen to devote her professional life to. A long, painstaking procedure that had moments when it seemed like the most extraordinary thing any doctor could do.

To remove such a vital organ and have a tiny chest open in front of you that had an empty space where the heart should be.

To take another heart and fill that space.

And, best of all, to join it up to every vessel and allow blood to fill it and, with the encouragement of a small, electric shock, to see it begin to beat and pump that blood around its new body.

It had taken a little over five hours from the time Penny's chest had been opened until the final stitches were in place and Rebecca stood back, as yet unaware of her aching back and feet, simply watching the monitor screen for a minute. The green light of the trace was a normal, steady rhythm. Blood pressure and oxygen saturation and every other parameter being measured were all within normal limits.

There were some tears again now, from more than one person in Theatre One, but they were happy tears. This little girl had the chance of a new future. As Rebecca allowed the intrusion of personal thoughts to mix with this overwhelming professional satisfaction, the joy of the potential new future became her own, as well. Looking up, the surprise this time was that Thomas had vanished from the gallery but Rebecca was smiling as she stripped off her mask and gown and gloves and left the theatre.

She knew she would find him waiting for her just outside the doors.

Waiting to fold her into his arms?

He came with her to find the space where Julia and Peter Craig were waiting.

'It's good news,' were the first words they heard. 'Everything went as well as we could have hoped for. Penny has a new heart.'

There were still more tears then. Both Penny's parents needed time to cope with the onslaught of relief and then allow themselves real hope. There were lots of questions to be answered again.

'Where is she now?'

'In Recovery. You'll be able to see her very soon.'

'Where will she go then?'

'Into Cardiac Intensive Care—like last time. We'll keep her asleep for a few days while we make sure the new heart is working perfectly. She'll probably be in there for seven to ten days.'

'And then...?'

'And then we'll move her back to the ward and Dr Wolfe will take over to keep a very close eye on things, but in two or three more weeks, we fully expect you to be taking Penny home.'

It was a long time later that Thomas and Rebecca finally left their young patient in the care of the very capable team in the cardiac intensive care unit. Neither of them could remember the last time they had eaten anything but it was too soon to do anything as mundane as finding a table in the staff cafeteria.

'Let's get a bit of fresh air,' Thomas suggested.

Rebecca shook her head. 'I can't leave the hospital. I need to be close to the unit for the rest of tonight. Besides, you know how many journalists and television crews are camped out in Reception. One interview was more than enough for me.'

'I'm amazed Penny's parents agreed to it.'

'I think they needed to say thank you. To everyone who helped to search for Penny. To the whole surgical team. And mostly, they wanted to let their donor's family know how much this gift means to them. They did that so well, didn't they? Even that woman who was interviewing us was crying.'

Rebecca's eyes were shining too brightly now, as well. She needed a bit of time away from everything.

'I know just the place,' Thomas told her. 'Come with me…'

He took her by the hand and led her up the stairs. Up and up, until they found themselves on the rooftop of Paddington Children's Hospital—just in time to see the last of a glorious summer sunset gilding the windows and chimneys of buildings and leaving the tops of the trees in their nearby parks a dark silhouette against a soft glow of pink.

'What a day…'

'I know.' Rebecca closed her eyes for a moment. 'I've never lost a patient when they were supposed to be on their way to Theatre before. I was so afraid Penny wasn't going to get her new heart.'

'But she did. Thanks to you. I can't tell you how proud I am of what you do, Becca. It's extraordinary. And brave, especially for you, but… but I think I understand *why* you do it, now.'

'*You* were brave,' Rebecca said softly. 'Being there for Ryan's surgery. I know how hard that must have been.'

'I'd just been with Ryan's parents. Talking to them.'

Rebecca's eyes widened. 'What did you say?'

'That they needed to believe they had been the best parents. That it was only because they loved their little boy so much that they were able to go through with giving the gift of life to others. That they should be there for each other and… and that they hadn't failed their son.'

'Oh, Tom…' Rebecca put her arms around him and pressed her forehead against his chest.

'That was when I *knew*,' he said. 'That we were the best parents, too. That what we did really is something to be proud of.' He kissed the top of Rebecca's head. 'I don't need to run any more. Or hide. I would never have chosen to get sucked back into the past the way Penny's case has taken me but it's the best thing that could have happened. I don't feel stuck any more.'

Rebecca lifted her head to meet his gaze. She opened her mouth but no words came out.

'We loved Gwen,' Thomas said softly. 'And we loved each other. And love that strong never dies, does it?'

'No, it never does.' Her voice wobbled. 'We'll always love Gwen. And remember her. And miss her.'

Thomas held her gaze. 'We will always miss her and we can't change that but I've missed you, too. I had no idea how much and I can't bear the thought of always missing you when that's something we *could* change. I love you, Becca. I need you—as much I need my next breath.'

'I love you, too, Tom. More than I ever have. You're still the person I fell in love with but there's so much more of you to love now. So many new layers. We've been through so much, haven't we?'

'We're older.' Thomas smiled. 'And wiser.' He dipped his head to place a gentle kiss on Rebecca's lips. 'But you're still the person I fell in love with, too. Just…more beautiful, inside and out.'

He kissed her again and, this time, there was passion to be kindled from within the tenderness. A promise of what was to come.

'I think I learned something important today,' he whispered, when they finally drew apart.

'I know you did.' Rebecca smiled. 'You learned not to hide.'

'And something else.'

'What?'

'That just because you didn't do something perfectly the first time doesn't mean that you failed.

It means you can learn something so you can do it better the next time.'

A tiny frown appeared between Rebecca's dark eyes. 'But you know you didn't fail with Gwen. *We* didn't fail…'

'I failed our marriage.'

'We both did.' The frown disappeared and there was a new glow in her eyes. 'But do you mean that you think we could do it better if there was a next time?'

'Not *if…*' Thomas paused to kiss Rebecca again. '*When.* If you'll say yes? Will you, Becca? Will you marry me again?'

'Yes,' she whispered. 'Yes and yes and yes!'

Maybe there would have been more 'yes's' but Thomas didn't need to hear any more.

Besides, he was too busy kissing her.

EPILOGUE

THIS WAS GOING to be an evening that nobody would ever forget.

'Oh, my goodness!' Rebecca had to pause for a moment to take in the scene through the doors ahead of them and Thomas smiled down at her.

'It's a bit of a step up from the Frog and Peach, isn't it?'

'Are you kidding? This is the *Ritz...*'

The magnificent dining room of the famous hotel looked like it belonged in a palace. A halo of chandeliers hung beneath the ceiling frescoes and the soft light glinted on the crystal and silver on the tables. Nobody had expected such a gala party to celebrate the official success of the campaign to save Paddington Children's Hospital but, once again, the generosity of people whose lives had been significantly touched over the many decades that the central London hospital had existed had resulted in an extraordinary donation.

So, here they were—a large group of the people who had been most involved in the campaign had been invited to gather and enjoy an evening to celebrate. They were all dressed in the kind of evening wear that befitted the programme of cocktails, dinner and dancing, along with speeches that would publicly acknowledge the contributions they had all made. The men's black tie outfits were a perfect foil to the splashes of colour in the gorgeous dresses some of the women had chosen to show off.

Rebecca had gone for a classic black dress, however. Maybe because it wasn't the dress that she wanted to show off. Glancing down, she straightened the fingers of her left hand. A tiny movement, but Thomas's smile broadened.

'How long will it be before anyone notices, do you think?'

Rebecca smiled back. 'Let's find out, shall we?'

It didn't matter if nobody else noticed, she

thought as she took his hand and turned to follow him to where everyone was gathering for a cocktail before dinner. They both knew she was wearing it for the first time and that it had a special significance. It wasn't the same ring Thomas had given her the first time she had agreed to marry him but it was the same solitaire diamond that had been reset—because they both wanted to keep the best of the old but make a new start.

'Can I offer you the cocktail menu?' a waiter queried. 'Or do you know what you'd like already?'

'A champagne cocktail, please,' Thomas said. 'There's a lot to celebrate tonight.'

'Just mineral water for me,' Rebecca said. 'I'm the sober driver.'

'Och, I've got one of those, too.' The voice behind her with its distinctive Scottish burr sounded amused.

She turned, with a grin, to greet Paddington's paediatric trauma surgeon, Dominic MacBride.

'Not for much longer, Dominic.' Her smile included the woman standing beside him. 'I wasn't sure you'd even make it tonight, Victoria.'

'It's crazy, isn't it? This baby seems to be determined to stay put for as long as possible.' Victoria's eyes widened as she watched Rebecca take the tall glass of water from the silver tray. 'Is *that* what I think it is on your finger?'

Rebecca's smile felt misty now. 'Yes. Tom and I are engaged. Again...'

'I knew it.' Alistair North turned his head towards them from where he and Claire were standing with Leo and his fiancée, Rosie, and Matt McGrory and his fiancée, Quinn Grady. 'I had a feeling something was going on that night when you were so late at the Frog and Peach you both missed the first party. You thought so, too, didn't you, Matt?'

'It was obvious,' Matt agreed. 'Just a matter of time.'

'Oh, congratulations—this is awesome news.' Claire stepped closer to admire Rebecca's ring. 'Are you going to have a big wedding or just duck into a registry office like Alistair and I will?'

'We haven't got round to planning anything,' Rebecca said. 'But it's second time around so I imagine we'll keep it pretty low-key.'

'Low-key...' Rosie sounded wistful. 'You wouldn't believe the amount of organisation that goes along with getting married to an Italian duke. Not that I'm complaining or anything...' The smile she gave Leo suggested that it was all very well worth it.

'We haven't got round to planning anything, either.' Dominic sighed. 'And it's not going to happen until this little princess decides to make her appearance.'

Victoria looked down at her impressive belly. 'Hear that?' she said. 'Daddy's getting impatient and I need to be able to wear a dress that doesn't look like a circus tent. It's time to make a move.'

'The sooner, the better,' Dominic added.

Thomas laughed. 'Be careful what you wish for,' he warned. 'Unless you want to avoid all the speeches tonight?'

'I reckon the dancing will do something,' Victoria said. 'And that won't be until all the speeches are finished.'

'Good luck with that.' Rebecca smiled. 'It didn't work for me and we tried a pretty fast salsa when Gwen was due.'

A sudden silence fell amongst the group of colleagues as some cautious glances were exchanged.

Rebecca and Thomas shared a glance of their own.

'It's okay,' Rebecca said. 'You all know our story and we know that you've all been so careful not to say anything but things have changed...' She felt the touch of Thomas's hand as his fingers curled around hers. 'Our first child will always be a very special part of our lives and we want to be able to remember her. And talk about her...'

'*First* child?' Claire was standing close enough to Rebecca to lower her voice and still be heard. 'And is that water you're drinking—like me?'

'Oh, look...' Rosie didn't seem to have heard the quiet comment. 'There's a film crew setting up over there. I didn't think this was going to be televised.'

'Maybe Sheikh Idris and Robyn are making a grand arrival. He's one of the biggest stars here tonight, after all. Without his donation, the campaign might not have been anything more than a protest.'

'No… I don't think so.' Rosie was peering through gaps as people started moving towards the dining tables. 'It's… Good heavens! Is that Julia and Peter Craig—Penny's parents?'

Rebecca nodded. 'There's an ongoing documentary being made about Penny's journey as a transplant patient. It all began the day of her surgery when she went missing and the crew happened to be there to catch the action. Everybody wanted to know what was happening and how things turned out.'

'I was one of them,' Victoria said. 'I was glued to my phone in the ultrasound waiting room, trying to get the latest news.'

'She became the poster girl for saving Paddington's in those last days, didn't she?' Claire added.

'So many headlines. I read somewhere that that was the final pressure needed to get everything signed and sealed.'

'But why are they still following her? Surely the family's got enough to cope with—it's not that long since her surgery.'

'I think Julia and Peter look at it as a way to give back,' Thomas said. 'They want to do all they can to raise awareness of the shortage of organ donors.'

'The committee invited them as special guests tonight,' Quinn put in. 'They *did* become so important as the finale to our campaign. And they're representing all the parents who owe so much to what Paddington's has been able to do.'

'And Penny's doing so well,' Rebecca added. 'I think they're delighted to share that. She's started back at school part time already. And she's started having ballet lessons.'

'Oh...' Rosie looked as if she was blinking back tears. 'That's the best news ever. I'd love to see her dancing.'

'I expect you will—on the documentary. Oh,

there's Idris and Robyn arriving and it looks like the official party's going in. That's our CEO, Dennis Bradley, with them. Hadn't we better go and find our table?'

There was a long table at one end of the room where the dignitaries like the CEO, people from Paddington's Board of Trustees and government officials were seated. Idris and Robyn were also at this top table, along with Julia and Peter Craig, but other guests were seated at round tables for six.

Thomas and Rebecca sat with Leo and Rosie and Matt and Quinn. The other tables quickly filled and a silence eventually fell as the Member of Parliament most closely associated with Paddington's stood up to say something. It was a short speech to start the evening where he welcomed everybody, thanked the owner of the Ritz hotel and Sheikh Idris Al Khalil for making this evening possible and finally offered a succinct toast.

'To Paddington Children's Hospital.'

The toast echoed throughout the room as

glasses were raised and then a new buzz of conversation broke out. It wasn't often that these colleagues got together socially and none of them were short of things to talk about.

'I can see Robyn's engagement ring from here,' Rebecca said to Rosie. 'It's no wonder she can't wear it at work.'

'I love that she's wearing a dress that's the same green as the emeralds in that ring. And doesn't she look happy?'

'Over the moon happy. I think I'd be exhausted by all that commuting she's doing. I'll bet she can't wait for the wedding and her final move to Da'har. And what about you guys? Didn't I hear that you're moving to Rome?'

'We've decided Florence is better,' Rosie told her. 'Leo's *palazzo* is in Tuscany, and we want to be near his mum.' Her voice trailed off as her attention was caught by Leo, who had been talking to Matt and Thomas but was now frowning at the screen of his phone. 'What's up, Leo?'

'I might just pop out for a moment.'

'Why?'

'I thought I'd ring the babysitter and check on the twins.'

'They're fine. She'd ring us if there were any problems. They'll both be sound asleep by now.'

'I'll just text her, then.'

Rosie shook her head. 'You know what, Leo?'

'What?'

'You're turning into a helicopter parent.'

They both seemed to find this amusing. Quinn was smiling, too.

'Maybe it's something to do with jumping in the deep end as a new parent. Matt and Simon are pretty much inseparable these days. They came up with a joint proposal for me, would you believe? We'd gone out for a picnic and they were both kneeling on the rug while they got things ready and then Matt proposed and Simon told me that I had to say "yes" because he wanted two parents for when he got properly adopted. And then they made me call Maisie and it turned out they'd tied my engagement ring to her collar.'

'Oh, that's so romantic. A real family proposal.'

'Mmm... What about yours, Rebecca?' Rosie

had turned back as Leo put his phone away. 'Was it a romantic proposal?'

'Of course it was.' Thomas had overheard the question. 'A perfect sunset and a view of half of London.'

Rebecca laughed. 'We were on the rooftop of Paddington's—near the helipad.' Then her laughter faded into a smile that was purely for Thomas. 'But yes, it was as romantic as I could have wished for.'

'I know what you mean about jumping in the deep end as a parent,' Rosie said to Quinn. 'You should see Leo. I don't even get a look in as the reader of bedtime stories any more. Apparently I'm nowhere near as good at doing dinosaur voices.'

Laughter and stories continued as the dinner service began. The food served that evening was as amazing as everybody expected, with dishes that featured treats like Norfolk crab, roasted scallops, venison and veal. Dessert delights included a praline custard and a banana soufflé. The three courses of the dinner were separated by speeches and many people were asked to stand and be acknowledged—like Quinn, at their table, for her contribution to the campaign committee. Rebecca missed the last bit of the pre-dessert course speech, however. It was the smell of the banana soufflé that was suddenly too much.

'Are you okay?' Rosie asked. 'You've gone very pale.'

'Bit warm, maybe.' Rebecca fanned herself with her menu, fighting off what appeared to be her first wave of morning sickness. 'Excuse me for a moment...'

With her hand pressed to her mouth, she tried to maintain a dignified walk to the restroom and not break into a run. She was aware that Thomas was following her but there was no time to wait for him.

She only just made it. And when she emerged from the cubicle to splash some cold water on her face, there was someone else doing the same thing at the neighbouring basin.

'I was right, wasn't I?' Claire's smile was rueful. 'How far along are you?'

'We only just found out,' Rebecca said. 'It's too early to tell anybody yet.'

'Your secret's safe with me.' Claire reached for one of the soft handtowels. 'I should be over this after three months, but maybe it's worse when it's twins…'

The door opened and Victoria came in. She was looking as pale as both the other women.

Claire and Rebecca looked at each other.

'I don't think you've got a problem with morning sickness, have you?'

Victoria sank onto the edge of one of the upholstered armchairs in this luxurious restroom.

'I just needed to move. Those straight dining chairs were giving me the most awful backache.' She closed her eyes and blew a long breath out through pursed lips. 'That's better. It's wearing off, I think.' Opening her eyes she smiled at the others.

'Don't mind me. I'll be fine. Go back and enjoy your dessert.'

Except that almost immediately her face tightened into lines of pain again and she bent her head, her arms clasped around her belly.

'I'll stay with her,' Rebecca murmured to Quinn. 'Can you go and get Dominic?'

The door swung shut behind Claire, only to open again almost instantly.

Thomas looked concerned. 'Claire told me that it looks like Victoria's in labour. Shall I call an ambulance?'

'Yes,' said Rebecca.

'No,' Victoria said at the same time. 'It's a first baby—nothing's going to happen in that much of a hurry. I just need to go to the loo…'

'Not a good idea,' Rebecca said.

'Ohhh...' Victoria gripped the upholstered arms of the chair. 'That hurts!'

The door opened again and Dominic came in. One look at Victoria and his jaw dropped. He reached for his phone. 'I'll call an ambulance.'

'I'm not sure there's time.' Victoria's voice was strained. 'This is crazy but… I think I have to push!'

'Hang on a tick. Let's just check what's happening first. Tom? Can you take her other arm? Let's get her onto the floor.'

Claire poked her head around the door and saw what was happening.

'Oh, heck… I'll stay out here and make sure nobody else comes in, shall I?'

'Please,' Thomas said. 'And call an ambulance. We're going to need some transport very soon.'

It was Dominic who lifted the folds of Victoria's dress out of the way. Thomas knelt behind her so that she could lean on him and Rebecca was holding her hand—or rather, letting her own hand get squeezed in a painfully hard grip.

'What's going on?' Victoria gasped. 'Can I push?'

'There's no cord in the way.' Dominic's voice was shaky. 'And she's crowning. Go for it, hon…'

It only took two pushes and a beautiful baby girl was delivered straight into her father's hands. The first, loud cry of the healthy newborn made Victoria burst into tears. Dominic had tears running down his own face as he put their daughter into her mother's arms and against her skin. Rebecca gathered every soft towel she could find on the shelves to cover them both for warmth and Thomas moved to let Dominic take his position and support his new family. Dominic's hands were shaking as he took his phone out of his pocket.

'Not that we're ever going to forget this,' he said. 'But could you do the honours?'

So Thomas took the very first family photo. Victoria lay against Dominic's chest and he was leaning over her shoulder as they both gazed down at a tiny face with wide open eyes that were staring back at her parents.

Thomas had to clear his throat as he handed back the phone. 'The ambulance should be here in no time.' He caught Rebecca's gaze and she nodded. This brand new family needed a little bit of time all to themselves.

'We'll be just outside the door if you need any help before then.'

Claire was guarding the door on the other side and had Alistair beside her but a small crowd had gathered behind them.

Robyn and Idris were there. And Rosie and Leo, Matt and Quinn.

'We heard her cry,' Rosie said. 'Is everything all right?'

Thomas put his arm around Rebecca's waist and drew her close to his side. 'Everything's perfect,' he said.

It seemed like every couple there needed to draw each other close as they shared the joy of this unexpected event. To smile. To touch. To steal a kiss…

Rebecca leaned closer to Thomas and looked up to bask in the intimacy of eye contact.

'That will be us in the not-too-distant future,' she whispered.

'I can't wait,' Thomas murmured back. 'You?'

Rebecca smiled. 'Like you said…everything's perfect…'

And it was.

* * * * *